THE NAMING OF GHOSTS

The Naming
of Ghosts

Thanks
Ron!

May the beauty
that we love be
what we do.

Stories by

~~Steve Mitchell~~

STEVE MITCHELL

Press 53
Winston-Salem

Press 53, LLC
PO Box 30314
Winston-Salem, NC 27130

First Edition

Copyright © 2012 by Steve Mitchell

Cover design by Kevin Morgan Watson

Cover art, "Working on a Dream," Copyright © 2012
by Peter Tandlund, used by permission of the artist.

Author photo by Christine Kirouac

Library of Congress Control Number: 2012935959

Printed on acid-free paper
ISBN 978-1-935708-56-8

Grateful acknowledgment is made to the publications where these stories first appeared:

"Dandelion," *The Adirondack Review*

"Ten-Year Stare," *The Press 53 Spotlight Anthology 2011*

"Wednesday," *Two Hawks Quarterly*

"Flare," *The Southeast Review*

"Vertigo Run," *Peregrine*

"Platform," *The North Carolina Literary Review*

"Margin," *Straylight Magazine*

"Wave," *Able Muse*

"Rose & Thistle," *Taking Flight: Winston Salem in Prose and Poetry*

"Roadside Tombstone," *moonShine review*

"Trouble in Mind," *Licking River Review*

"Home" and "Above the Rooftop," *Contrary Magazine*

The Naming of Ghosts

Dandelion

I dreamt his dream again. He was sleeping soundly, warm beside me, and I dreamt his dream; opening my eyes with a start but no sound, opening my eyes without moving. Shocked into place.

With only the hush of breathing. Not his. Not quite mine. The breathing which has become a part of us, settled into every inch of our lives. The breathing which reminds.

Because the past can become so real that I get loose in time and don't know where I am and it takes something to snap me into place, something to call me forward again, so I can lie beside him in the dark, early hours of morning, feeling the heat of our knowing under the blankets all around me, and realize for a moment where I am.

Soon, I'll get up and make coffee, leaving the couch to Jim alone. I'll sit in the kitchen to drink it, watching the light ease into the trees, then the sky, outside the window. The world will take shape around me and the dream will fade and I'll only be vaguely aware of the breathing, still present, low and even. For now, I let the dream circle inside me, clacking like a pinball from one organ to the next, one thought to the next. I let the dream have its due.

We had left the party early. The night was clean and humid after a summer rain and we wanted to claim our own time. Jim was driving and I was leaning into him, my head resting on his shoulder, my lips at his neck.

His hand had drifted along my thigh, under my dress, and his fingers turned there, out of sight, stroking waves of heat into my flesh. We were working to get further into each other's skin. We were catapulting home on our own rail, rushing to arrive before our bodies exploded into each other, there in the front seat of the car.

His fingers slowly stirred a gear, angling deeper inside me, my hand on his chest, my mouth half-open at his neck, his neck warm with the scent of the rain and cigarettes smoked long ago. The car whistled through the slick night: a part of our world, the definition of our world; the shell delivering us home. Home to each other.

His head tilted, his mouth angling toward my ear, and he whispered something. Now I can't remember what it was. I remember his breath building there and the gentle hum of his voice, but not the actual words themselves. And we felt the car hit something. Something slight, a glancing blow. We felt it before we heard it.

"What was that?" I straightened in the seat and Jim brought both hands to the wheel, his foot instinctively lifting from the accelerator.

"I don't know. A branch, maybe. A squirrel."

"Do you think we ought to go back?"

The road was black, even and empty, and Jim didn't bother to pull off to the shoulder. He eased the car to a stop in the lane and we sat there for a few seconds, Jim staring forward through the misted windshield while I studied the road behind, the wet asphalt tinged red in the glow of the taillights.

"It might be a cat," I suggested, "or someone's dog. It might be hurt."

"Yeah, you're right," he replied with a sigh.

Jim accelerated slowly, turning the car in the road, the front wheel bumping off the shoulder then back onto the asphalt. He turned the car again 500 feet up and brought it to the edge of the pavement, creeping forward, the headlights throwing a yellow pale into the trees a few feet from the road.

We inched along, staring hard into the thick wet underbrush and spreading branches. Jim's hand had returned to my knee and I laced my fingers into his. Finally he found a slight opening in the underbrush where an animal might have darted. He slowed the car to a stop and we got out. I had forgotten how thick and warm the night had become. The dew in the air was nearly visible.

Jim was in front of me in the break of underbrush and I bumped into him when he stopped.

"Oh, my God," he whispered.

He raised his arm to hold me back but I pushed past him, without thinking, and nearly stumbled over her.

In the dream, the woman is naked; in the dream I can see her broken bones beneath the skin, the blood filling the cavity of her lungs. In the dream, I cannot remember her face but I am surrounded by the wet green of the high trees and the rasp of her short, shallow breaths.

She was older, in her late forties or fifties, with thin, light hair lying close to her skull. She was wearing rain galoshes unbuckled at the top and a yellow rubber raincoat thrown open to reveal a chenille housecoat over a loose fitting floral dress. Her legs were folded slightly to the left and one arm had been thrown above her head, as if her body were in the midst of a single ecstatic leap.

In the dream, she turns, there upon the wet leaves, in a slow spin which never ends, but on that night she lay completely, inescapably, still. I knelt down beside her, Jim stumbling up behind me, and reached out to touch her cheek.

"Emma," Jim said, his voice frightened and uncertain.

"It's okay," I told him, without knowing what I meant.

There was no blood. Her face was deeply lined, her skin pale and loose. Her lips shuddered with the quick, labored breaths. Her eyes were low slits beneath the eyelids. She was cool and wet.

"We have to get help," Jim said, his voice stronger and more centered now.

"I'll stay here," I told him.

Jim knelt beside me and took the woman's wrist, searching for her pulse, then his hand came to my shoulder gently.

"There's nothing you can do here."

He helped me up and we moved quickly toward the car, my knees and dress dripping, my hands trembling. "I think there's a gas station a couple of miles ahead," I told him, "Of all the times not to have my phone." The break in the underbrush was larger when I looked back, the high weeds broken and dangling.

A mile and a half down the road, Jim began to slow the car. It had come to a stop again before I noticed.

"Emma," he whispered, turning to me in the seat, "we can't tell anyone."

"What do you mean?" I stammered.

"We can't tell anyone. Don't you see what it would mean?" His voice was low, he was staring at his hands. "We've been drinking, we've been to a party. It would mess everything up. The police."

"Jim," I was crying now, "We can't just leave…"

Jim leaned in close and placed his hand over mine, "I felt her pulse, Emma. It won't make any difference."

We are home already, making love on the floor in front of the sofa. A half-empty bottle of wine rests upon the coffee table beside two abandoned glasses. There is a single candle burning high in the window and the night is dark and calm. My fingers stroke the curve of Jim's shoulder.

We are lifting her into the car. I am pushing the door wider with my body, sliding her legs in first along the back seat. Jim is at her shoulders, speaking softly, reassuring her, as we arrange her along the width of the seat. We find a blanket in the trunk to keep her warm.

We are sitting, talking, in the front seat with the car idling, the windows fogging around us. There is not another car on this road. Jim is talking about finishing med school. He's talking about what our life could be. I say something about accidents.

"There was nothing we could do, Emma," Jim whispers, drawing me toward him, "she's probably dead already."

And she was dead by the time the paramedics arrived. Emily Barstow lived alone in a small house not far from the highway. The police knew her well, as she often called them to complain of aliens landing in her backyard or stood on the shoulder of the road berating cars as they passed. The short newspaper article stated that Ms. Barstow had been arrested on numerous occasions for public drunkenness and had spent several months at the State Mental Hospital.

I had convinced Jim to stop at a phone booth so I could call the ambulance anonymously but, by the time they arrived, she was already dead. The newspaper article didn't help me to know her any better. The texture

of her skin and sound of her fading breath told me all I
needed to know.

Six months later, I found myself on the bathroom floor
at two in the morning. Jim was off, cramming for exams
with friends, and I couldn't keep any food down. I had
awakened from the dream again, twisted tight around
the sheets, bile rising into my dry throat.

I lay naked at the base of the toilet after vomiting,
waiting for the next cramp to come. The floor was a hard,
cold white rising into the mouth of the toilet and my
feet slipped along its surface as I lifted myself to vomit
again. I bent low into the bowl, the cramp pushing fluid
from my nose and mouth, acrid burning water, which
splashed back into my face. I tensed around the cramp,
pressing my body at the waist, pressing hard. I wanted
it out, I wanted it all out.

I lay my cheek along the porcelain rim. It was cold
beneath my face where the sweat had dried. I was trying
to breathe as my stomach lurched. My legs were curling
under me, my body closing in on itself.

There was another breath in the room pushing down
upon me. I could feel its rhythm and its rustle all around
me. My own breath was ragged in my lungs and it
would not stay there, it would not settle. As if the body
purging itself of all food was now purging itself of air. I
struggled, raising myself upon my elbows along the cold
floor, gasping for breath, a jagged panic beginning to
churn in my stomach.

I pursed my lips and tried to exhale in a slow and steady
stream, afraid of hyperventilating, afraid my bronchia were
tightening in some weird kind of anaphylactic shock. I tried
to slow my breathing but nothing happened and my lungs
were slowly closing; I could feel them tighten, I could hear
the air whistling through the narrowing spaces.

The panic became electric and my arms flung themselves outward, grasping for anything, slamming the tiled wall and white floor, my bloodied knuckles leaving thin red scars along the tiles. I wheezed and struggled. The other breath was there, slow and steady, around me; trying to enter, trying to force its way through. I heard its rhythm beneath my anguished, constricted gasps. It pressed itself at my lips, it pushed its way into my mouth.

I fought it, lying flat upon the floor, slapping my palms against the tiles, the crisp shock cracking from the walls. I fought it until there was no breath of my own left, until my lungs folded in upon themselves, loose as a paper sack, and I wheezed empty, my eyes glazing, my fingers twitching on the floor.

Then, it entered me, bringing its own rhythm; it filled my lungs softly. It filled them completely and my body relaxed, all at once, each cell awakening. I began to cry, naked, on my back, staring into the white ceiling. I cried and gave myself to the new breath. I cried, the tears streaking the sides of my face, drying there, then streaking again until pools formed in my ears. The breathing slowed within me so completely that I thought I was dead.

Then, I threw myself forward, clutching the toilet bowl, and vomited until I was certain there was nothing left.

All pain is secret; that is its power and its limit. This pain was once a single tight stem but it has blossomed. The hurt, the ache and guilt, then burst outward around the center, becoming larger and more beautiful, forming a sunburst mist in which I could see every tendril, every thread and synapse. It bloomed into a perfect sphere, trembling, waiting only for a breeze to loosen each thin stalk.

With my new breath, I blew gently into the sphere. Once I had healed; once my knuckles were no longer bruised and my stomach eased, once my ribs no longer ached and I could sleep. The breath loosened each spore and they took flight, blowing through me, seeding the pain and taking root throughout my body, penetrating every cell.

Two years later, I am packing boxes and we are moving from the small med-student ghetto apartment, across town, to a house with a yard, to be near Jim's practice and the law office where I work. The years here have accumulated all kinds of things, but I'm packing it all and taking it all with us. I know some boxes will be unpacked later and some will simply be shoved into the attic or basement and not disturbed for years.

At first, Jim and I tried to talk about the accident. In hushed, urgent tones, for weeks after, we tried to make sense of what we had done. But after a time, each exchange fell into the same grooves and we found ourselves repeating lines we didn't understand or believe. Eventually, each conversation faded simply into silence or halted whenever Jim said, "Some things are best forgotten."

I think we had always dreamt together; it took the accident to bring it out. We continued to talk about the dreams for weeks after we had stopped talking about the accident; sorting our own images one from the other, and the spaces where they grew thin or overlapped. The dreams were not real, they were imaginary, and that made them cleaner, safer. Soon, we stopped talking about the dreams also, but Jim continued to turn and ache in his sleep and I eventually found myself on the bathroom floor.

His dreams sunk deeper, so deep he could no longer recognize them; while mine kept rising to the surface until they were finally indistinguishable from the world around me and pressed in upon me so strenuously that I threw up. Again and again.

I had Delacorte, though, and I could always talk to her. We had been students together and, while we didn't work at the same law firm, the two were close enough to each other that we could manage lunch on Fridays. The Friday lunch eventually transformed into a weekly dinner, our "dinner meeting."

It was Delacorte who could make me laugh. With her ridiculous bug-eyed impressions of her co-workers, her outrageous gossip about the law partners. Her well-planned and idiosyncratic shopping trips, with me in tow, to some chic new uptown boutique housed in an old bus garage.

It was Delacorte who picked me up at work one afternoon and drove me to the beach. "No arguments," she explained, "just sit there and enjoy the ride. You can complain all you want on Thursday. Thursday is a good day for complaint. Today, however, you just gotta be quiet."

When we arrived at a strip of coastline secluded by a high dune and a short plateau of rock, she drew two flimsy lawn chairs from the trunk of her car and strode toward the water, planting each resolutely, side by side, a few feet from the surf. "Sit here," she commanded, "watch the sunset. You'll like it."

Soon, the sunset erupted over the clear horizon, threading itself into strata of pink and orange and gold, and it was beautiful. I enjoyed it, just as she said I would.

I was having dinner with Delacorte earlier in the evening, our usual dinner meeting, and she was talking about another paralegal at the practice whose increasingly shoddy work she constantly had to repair.

"I don't want to make a scene at the office but I don't

know how long this can go on before I just snap his neck and force his body through the paper shredder." She paused, a forkful of spinach salad near her mouth, and asked me, "Sooner or later, someone will notice, right? Sooner or later, one of the attorneys will see who's to blame.'"

My mind had been wandering but her pause drew me back. "Maybe it's not about blame," I told her as she chewed, "maybe, sometimes, we take responsibility for the people we love. Maybe that's a part of what love is."

Delacorte snorted, "Well, I certainly don't love Burnell!"

"I know," I smiled, then I tried to explain, "What I mean is, maybe you're responsible for what you see. And the people who don't see something, or can convince themselves they don't, maybe it's not their business. Maybe it's only the business of the ones who see."

"Lord," Delacorte exclaimed, thumping her tea glass on the table for emphasis, "that doesn't seem very fair."

"I know," I giggled. "It doesn't."

"Sometimes…" Delacorte sighed, shaking her head and pointing her finger at me, "sometimes you need a second glass of wine."

I knew Jim was dropping by the new house after work, to finish painting windows, so I was surprised when the lights were on in the apartment. I walked into the wreckage of the living room to find he had fallen asleep on the couch, surrounded by stacked and open boxes, thick wads of newspaper. Over the past weeks, he had hardly slept, dividing his time between the new practice and the house. Now, he was lying on his back, his mouth slack, one hand trailing on the floor.

Beside him, on the top of a closed box by the couch was a small gold foil packet of chocolates, a single red rose and a scrawled note which simply said, "I tried to wait up…"

I knelt by the couch and whispered into Jim's ear; he turned onto his side without waking, to face the back of the couch. I took off my clothes and lay down beside him, spooning into the curves of his body, my arm sliding along his chest and coming to rest there. I enjoyed the texture of his clothes against my bare skin.

Jim still tossed at night, wrapping the sheet around his body, sometimes clutching the pillow, sometimes murmuring. Often, in sleep, his body felt taut, a fluttering voltage pulsing just beneath the skin. But tonight his muscles had loosened, his face had gone slack. My fingers dusted the features of his cheek and shoulder. I fell asleep beside him and awakened, with a start, to the dream.

In the dream now, she spins, winding herself in a fine, translucent thread. I watch her turn for a long time; her face relaxed, her chest hardly moving. The thread winds around her, glistening like a spider web in the dew, until it begins to cover her, swaddling her within a silvered cocoon. This turning slows until the cocoon ceases its spin and drops slowly to the damp leaves.

I turn onto my back, fresh from the dream, half on and half off of the couch. Jim is at my side, his breathing slow and even. He sounds peaceful, calm; deep in the arms of night.

I'm thinking of the night in the car, his easy touch along my leg and the simple heat between us. I am watching the earth hurtle by us in wet, green streams outside the window, fading into darkness as soon as we pass. I'm remembering his smell then, on that damp night.

We are already settled, with good jobs and a modest house. We have breakfast together every morning and drink our coffee slowly, imagining our day or studying the sharpening shadows on the blonde wood of the kitchen table.

We are explaining the accident to a policeman and he understands our fear and our concern. He listens to us intently, prompting us with the occasional question. Then, he leads us to a room where we sit together, waiting, while they type our statement.

We are lying together on the daybed by the big window, naked, a single cool sheet over us. A storm is raging through the night outside and the rain and occasional leaves whip against the panes. We are not making love. It is before, or it is after. We are holding each other close.

I dream the dream for him. I hold a space open, a place he could step into at any time, a self I keep alive for him. I dream the dream so he can sleep.

Ten-Year Stare

It was a look I seen and I seen it true. Then I forgot it 'til I seen it again then I remembered it. All of it. Every minute in the between and that one on each end.

Like memory comes full circle pulling a kind of noose round my neck slow, tightening from the first look to the last. For a second then I seen into his world. We were together then for a second. And it felt alright. Clear. I could see the inside of the noose where the air was. And inside the noose it's light blue. The color of a finished sky.

Before. He'd been sittin' on the floor in the living room of the trailer, his trucks and cars all around him. This was before his mom left, before everything started to rust. And I was mad about somethin' or I'd been drinkin' or I was just a son of a bitch or he was a pain in the ass but I told him to clean that stuff up and get it out of the floor and he just kept right on and I reached down and jerked him up by the arm and slapped him hard and dropped him again right there on the floor.

He didn't cry. I think I scared him more than hurt him. He laid all balled up on the floor there and he looked up at me, them blue eyes big. I thought he'd hate me but that wasn't what I seen. I wished it hada been hate. But it weren't. It was like I'd disappeared. He just looked right through me like he already seen a time when I was gone. He rubbed his face. He looked right through me. Then he started pickin' up his toys. That was then.

His momma she was working down at the convenience store then and I thought he'd tell her when she come home. Thought he'd come whimperin' in to her his bottom lip all stuck out, hours later like it'd just happened. They did stuff like that, him and her; come back at you with somethin' you done long after you already forgot about doing it. That woman'd get in my face now and again and my brain'd be whirrin', spinnin' back, tryin' to find what it was she was talking about.

Anyway, he didn't tell her. Just climbed in her lap when she lit her cigarette and sat down, climbed up there and clung to her like a little monkey.

I mean, it ain't me he should be all mad at anyhow. She's the one that left us. Came home from the plant one evenin' and he's sitting on the cinder block step out in front of the locked door. School bag on the ground beside him. He's readin' a magazine he got at school and she's gone. We know it soon as we open up the door and that goddamn ugly ceramic clock ain't on the kitchen counter where she put it the day she brought it home. I hated that damn clock.

He come in dragging his book bag behind him, looked around the living room and kitchen for a second then sat down on the couch and kept lookin' through his magazine. I lit a cigarette and sat down next to him and we just sat there awhile. Him readin', me smokin'. Then we went out to Hardee's for dinner.

It's her he should hate. Not me.

Maybe he does hate her. I wouldn't know. He's a goddamn mystery to me.

Living's just a blur, you know. A whir you feel streakin' by like cars on a highway while all the time the edges are pullin' in tighter just outta sight and the space around you is gettin' smaller and smaller, pushin' the air outta itself. It's hard to know what I did and what I didn't do.

One day don't bleed into the next. There ain't no difference between days so there's nothin' to bleed into or out of. I'd come home from the plant or from drinkin' or from just being away and he'd be fine. He'd a made himself a sandwich and be all curled up on the couch or his bed with a book or a magazine. Weren't no kids to play with, trailer too far back off the road, but he found things to do.

Living's just a blur, you know, it all runs together. It's hard to know what I did and didn't do. He never said nothin' about it. He'd come in from school or wherever he'd been outside and not say nothin' about the night before. He got quieter and quieter. Days we hardly saw each other which was fine with me. While he got bigger that goddamn trailer got smaller and smaller. Further back in them goddamn woods.

Then one day there he was all nerve and bone. All six foot what-the-hell of him. And the trailer's cold and my back aches and I'm tired cause we're workin' overtime at the plant and I can't say no cause they're layin' people off and I'm tellin' him how things are gonna be and he gets himself up off that couch and he just looks at me. Looks at me for the first time in probly ten years.

And it's the look I already seen.

And all the news of the past spins out at me all at once. Suckin' the air outta the room, pullin' the noose tight around my neck. There ain't no blue left no more in the space inside the noose.

We were together then for a second. It'd been a long time. I could see him for a second and it was alright.

I stand in his way in front of the door but he just walks around me. Don't even look at me, he's all finished with lookin' at me. He just walks around. And he leaves. Leaves me in a place where there ain't no space to move around in and a lot of time to do it.

Screen door flappin' behind him. Slappin' itself against the hollow door frame. This trailer gettin' empty, and colder and colder.

Wednesday

Ana is listening. For the moment. She leans forward across the café table, one elbow planted upon its glassy surface, chin cupped in her hand. Her eyes anchored and blue, settling upon me, negating the existence of the surrounding world.

I am trying to tell her something. Explain it in my usual circuitous strands. Throwing out a number of threads at once, almost randomly, then attempting to weave them together into a delicate, yet resilient, fabric. More often than not, I simply watch the cloth unravel before my eyes.

I am trying to find a way to say something outside the range of words. Something which refuses to condense into syllables. I continue to speak, hoping perhaps that a music might bear my meaning. She is accustomed to these extemporaneous performances, comfortable with the tempo of my stutters and bumps.

"Does everything with you have to be some sort of declaration?" she asks finally, her lip curling to one side in the suggestion of a sneer. As if she doesn't know the answer.

"Not always," I attempt to take offense, "I can talk about groceries and plumbing without feeling the need to uncover the hidden."

"I don't know…" she replies, the sneer shifting to a knowing smile, "there's always a mystery or a secret."

"You're right," I sigh, pushing back into the corner of my chair, dropping my hands into my lap in surrender, "there are things I know and things I don't know and I get the two confused. The only way I can make things real sometimes is to proclaim."

"It's the passion that gets you…" she unfolds one slender hand upon the table, studying her fingertips, angling a glance in my direction, "I remember in high school, you were always railing about some issue, some injustice. There goes Sarah, marching toward the Great Objective Truth," Ana chuckles, closing her hand gently. "I liked it. You always seemed so sure."

"I'm not sure of much any more," I admit, lacing my fingers around my coffee cup, "must have something to do with having children…"

"…mortgage payments…"

"…retirement plans…"

"…neighborhood associations…"

We laugh, Ana sliding down in her seat, extending her tanned legs to the side of the table, resting her palms at its edge. We had finished lunch twenty minutes earlier, argued over dessert, dramatically convincing each other not to indulge. The dishes and napkins had been cleared. Now, we waste time over coffee. It is late afternoon and the waiters are either dozing behind the bar or smoking a joint in the alley.

I shift in my chair, trying to find a place for my feet beneath the table, my hands above, spinning loose in my own words. Ana has tilted her head toward the window and a band of sunlight frames her profile. Her peach colored blouse is open at the throat, a silver chain falling to her breasts.

"I wasn't sure of anything then," she remembers. She chuckles again, her voice low along the table, "I'm not sure of anything now. Come to think of it, I've never been sure of anything."

"It's just an act. A place you get yourself into. It doesn't mean anything. On the other hand…"

Ana's eyes spark, flickering blue light. "That's not quite true, you know. I say it but it's not quite true." Her hand churns the air between us, apologizing for the interruption while encouraging herself. "This memory just bloomed in my head, you know how memories can do that? All at once. One time in high school. I was at home with all this tissue paper spread out on the floor of my room and a big piece of poster board."

She leans far across the table toward me, her fingers tented beneath her chin; I edge forward to meet her. She is whispering, not in complicity, but tenderness.

"I was going to make something girly, you know, puffy paper flowers glued to the board. But I had a brush and somehow the paper got wet and dripped this big red splotch on my clean board. I thought I would cry. This drip had messed everything up, this blood-red drop. But I laid the red paper over it, just a strip, and then I wet it with the brush and the color bled out and then…"

Her voice is barely audible now, even though I am only an inch from her lips. The room has collapsed around us, the table beneath us; the light has formed a pool. It reminds me of the moments in old movies when they turn off the lights on the set one by one until someone stands alone in a single spot. Or, lying on the floor with three other girls during a sleepover, 2 a.m. and the entire world is asleep, only us awake and in those moments we can offer any secret, reveal the most delicate thoughts. Lying atop our Little Mermaid sleeping bags, head to head, in a teenage pinwheel, staring at the ceiling as each of us speaks. Sometimes we hold hands.

"…I wasn't sure I'd ever been that happy before. The deep red flag on the white paper was beautiful. The most beautiful thing I'd ever seen," Ana grabs my hand, a minute tremble underlying her skin, "and I suddenly realized that I had done that. Put the red on the paper. That before me it had not existed, that without me it would not exist."

Ana releases me, tracing the flank of my forearm with the fingers of her right hand, reluctant to sever contact. She draws a deep breath, allowing her gaze to settle on the table, as if studying now the colors upon the paper then. "I spent the rest of the afternoon pasting bits of tissue on the poster board, allowing the colors to run and mix with each other, laying one shade over another. As if I had never seen color before. Had just discovered it."

Her eyes rise from the table to meet mine, cobalt hot upon my face. "I believed in something then…don't know what it was," she draws herself erect in the chair, her low, sensuous laugh deep within her chest, raising her arms in a semblance of prayer, "…but I believed in it."

I don't want to speak, to break the spell of her memory, to lighten the rest of the room. I don't want her to stand up or move away. I want to spin around this common axis; to protect the warm enclosed space we have created through her speaking and my listening.

"I know what you mean…" I tell her, aware that my words are only a delay, a way of waiting, "watching Brittany paint, it's pure joy for her. There's nothing between her and the paint, the paper. She doesn't know, she's just playing, of course…"

Ana doesn't lean back in her chair, she doesn't pull away. She watches me, the smile curling at the edge of her mouth, revealing a top molar which had cracked when she was 21, requiring an emergency root canal. We had been on vacation together, our first alone. I had waited for her in the reception area, shivering in my bathing suit. Later, she had fallen, satiated with Darvocet, into a lawn chair at the edge of the surf, intent upon salvaging each remaining moment of the day. When darkness fell, I led her back to our room, arm in arm, her legs rubbery in the black sand.

I latch onto my coffee cup again, the contents cooling, the cream collecting in a suspicious ring around the inside edge. I take a sip, the coffee smoky and thick even with the cream and sugar, hours old.

Her hands come to rest upon the table, one over the other, yet her eyes never shift from mine. She wants something more than I have given her. She doesn't demand it; she isn't expecting a transaction of some sort. A level of mystery has been made real; not apparent, yet solid and tangible. She has given me a permission I haven't noticed. I resist the urge to glance around, to break the spell, to acknowledge a world larger than the two of us.

"I'm thirteen," I begin, fully committed from the start, "first period, three months before. Marinating in hormones. Molly Stewart is over at my house and, I don't know, we're getting ready to go to the Mall, or the movies or something. And we're trying on each other's clothes, the way we always did. The room looks like a bomb blast at The Gap. Nearly everything she owns and everything I own spread on the floor, the bed, everywhere.

"I turn around from the closet—I was grabbing another dress—and Molly's standing in the center of the

room completely naked. She's not provocative in any
way, she's just deciding what to put on next."

Ana brushes a strand of hair from her face and leans
forward. I realize I am the one whispering now, a ragged
heat trapped in my throat, leaving me hoarse and
breathless.

"I had seen naked girls before. Of course. Gym class,
sleepovers. It wasn't that. And Molly, she was like the
rest of us at thirteen, she didn't have much of a shape.
But she was in that place, you know, where she wasn't a
kid anymore but she wasn't a grown-up either. I was
just speechless. Creamy skin, red hair falling at her
shoulders, the field of freckles above her breasts, the
bend of her knee. She was incredible."

"What did you do?"

"Nothing," I shrug, "I tossed her the dress. She put
it on."

It is my turn to stare. I don't want to stare into the
distance, to create the space beyond us and allow it to
take physical form. So, I do what Ana had done; I stare
at my hands palms down upon the black lacquered
table. Midnight Surrender nail polish. Wedding ring.
The scar from the broken glass. The bracelet Brittany
had assembled from small shells.

Ana's hands are close to mine. I've always thought
hers prettier, more delicate. Elegant, tapering fingers,
skin the color of ivory. Her hands rest palms up in
anticipation of a gift which has not yet arrived.

I sigh, not knowing exactly why.

"Things like that don't have a reason," Ana whispers,
"I mean, they're just beautiful, they exist for themselves.
Joy doesn't leave anything behind but us."

Our hands upon the table; they lie at oblique angles
to each other; hers open, mine palms down. A humming
still life set against a black background, the narrow

parallel of our fingers offset by the white porcelain circles of our cups. Two women who had suffered college together, married within two years of each other, birthed children and shared playgroups. Some Wednesdays our conversation splashed in the shallow surf, all giggles and noise; but every now and then, we plunged together so far and so deep that we had difficulty orienting to shore.

She studies me, her head slightly bowed, hair falling from the sides in a fine, dark curtain. She peers up toward me over the rims of her round glasses, waiting patiently to catch my eye. I avoid her, folding my vision into my hands. I know this gaze; it's the one she used when I cried after failing Physics freshman year, when Rob Simons dumped me just before Spring Break, when my Mom went back home after Brittany's birth.

I feel her eyes calling me, though I refuse to meet them, resolutely training mine upon the table. She is patient. She is always patient. There is a stillness conspiring within her, fostering the conviction that she might pause before me forever, an endearing Sphinx. The bubble around us has the hushed quiet of new snow. We can't hold joy, only allow it.

I want to give Ana something; to place something delicate and precious within her open palm. I want to compile a catalogue of joy. It will be an index of sunlight, its texture and shape, its spectrum of warmth. Its infinite differing faces.

I'll assemble a book, as awkward as a teenager's tender diary, and present it to Ana. There will be snapshots and mementos. A worn blanket spread in the sun for a spring picnic with the children. Swarms of oily bubbles blown from plastic wands lifting to the trees. Ana filling my wine glass, our eyes following the lazy ripples on the lake. A ticket stub. A pink bow.

A silken story unfolding in unbroken swathes of color. I will catalogue my joy and make it my faith.

I look up into the archive of Ana's eyes. I see the single, gentle thread of my life. It whips like a wide banner in the breeze, a slash of deep color against a cloudless blue sky. I gasp. I gasp as the banner unfurls. I gasp and tell her something which is a mystery until it is spoken.

"I'm leaving my husband."

The world behind her flickers. A waiter shuffles in the shadows of the bar. I see chairs, booths, a large window opening to the street. Tables for other diners who have not yet arrived. Ana's eyes do not leave me; she wills the world to silence. I promise myself I will not cry.

"You need a place to stay?" she asks.

"Maybe," I reply.

Flare

She'd built the fire in the middle of the living room floor, between the coffee table and the overstuffed chair, not far from the television. By the time I stumbled in, the flames were pretty high and it was hard to tell whether she'd used my clothes or her own. I backed into the bedroom, still bleary eyed, pulling the comforter from the bed and running at the fire like a drunken matador. I fell toward the flames, wrestling them into the blanket, inhaling great gobs of smoke and blackening my hands, rolling on the floor with the flames until I was sure they'd died; then I sat up, straight legged in my pajamas, catching my breath by the smoldering mound of ash and comforter.

It was one of the great things about Evie, she was always surprising me. I never knew what she'd do next and I never seemed quite prepared for what she came up with. The chunks of glass in my iced tea, the razor blades in my shoes. The blue-black glint in her eye and her roundhouse swing. The fights melting into rapturous lovemaking, her body bucking under mine, arms pinwheeling her head, clutching at my shoulders or the bedsheets, her breath ragged in my ear; or, the disastrous sex, bruised and raw, giving way to a new bloodletting, always somehow unique, both of us managing to find new weapons or use old ones in new ways.

The smoke alarm finally clicked off and the silence surprised me. I looked up; everything else in the apartment seemed intact, only the front door was ajar. I got up to close it, running my fingers lovingly over the scarred doorframe and the pitted wall of the entrance hall, remembering how she'd shoved me to the floor by the door and mounted me there, my body wedged tightly into the corner; or how I'd ripped her blouse open from the back and pushed her onto the shapeless couch. Her teethmarks on my chest, the bruise on her neck.

I was scooping the smoking corpse of the fire into a metal trashcan I'd retrieved from my office when the doorbell rang. I let it ring while I finished the job, let it ring until it became a knock, tentative at first then more emphatic. His hand was in mid-air when I threw the door open.

He looked like an accountant or a coroner, all sandy-boyish hair and sweater vest. He blinked at me with an innocent confusion. I don't know whether it was my scorched pajamas or my sooty face. I studied him, imagining Evie standing over the bed as he slept, plotting his dismemberment.

"Evie sent me for her things," he said. Then, extending his hand, "I'm Adam."

"Yeah, I bet you are," I replied, shoving the smoldering trashcan into his arms and closing the door.

Evie. Man, I love that woman.

The Naming of Ghosts

I imagine the car idling low, nearly silent, its exhaust pluming then vanishing almost instantly in the January night; the car poised at the edge of the frozen lake, headlights throwing a grimy light upon the unmarked expanse of snow, throwing it out across the lake farther and farther until the light gives way to the night, the cold, the ice. I imagine him behind the wheel in the faint green-glow of the dashboard dials, his fifth or sixth cigarette clutched between yellowed fingers, the interior thick with smoke and old sweat, the floor strewn with empty cans. His tractor cap at a lazy slant, blue eyes clinging to a face webbed in smoke and liquor and living hard. I know the silence surrounding the low idle of the motor, the silence of the frozen trees hushed in snow, the motionless lake, the unforgiving darkness, the mist of ice still hanging in the air. I know the loneliness, the sense of isolation and the nearness to something indefinable. I imagine he stares into the cone of light before him for a very long time.

He had fished the lake a thousand times. I imagine he knew every inch, both in summer as in winter, because

he was a fisherman who saw the very presence of
weather as an existential challenge, a dare from God.
He knew where to find the fish, even in January. He
knew where the ice was thin. He knew the invisible
currents of warmth beneath the surface, the deer paths
and fox trails through the woods. He knew the rippling
seam where the water met the bank. The lake had been
his only axis, the one constant in his bruised and ragged
life. Over the years, in the weeks or months between
jobs, I imagine his car crawled the shoreline disgorging
butts and beer cans, in search of sanctuary, the daily
signs which might lead him to the largest and most
defiant catch or the most untroubled spot, far from the
weight of others. And some days, all he might do is
drive, down one pocked road after another, passing the
hours in constant motion. Away, always moving away.

He had a wife whom I had never met; a wife who, at the
funeral, appeared dumbfounded with either his life or
his death. I remember how she stood hunched and small
in the center of the bare room, expectant of some
understanding or revelation which never arrived. She
plucked at the hem of her blouse when not shaking an
outstretched hand. She hovered by the small picture
taken during a fishing trip years ago, his blue eyes
staring out, head cocked, cheeks rutted by time and sun
and cigarettes, an upraised beer just out of frame. Her
eyes shifted from the picture to the open door and it
was hard to say whether she was anticipating more
guests or planning her escape. She nodded in my
direction when I stepped reluctantly over the threshold
and smiled as if she knew me but I could have been
anybody. Our shoes squeaked on the white linoleum
floor in the high, arid silence of the room and she took
my hand into her bony palm whispering a distracted

thank you. And I joined her for a moment by the photo, trapped there like her within his vanishing wake. Later, I looked back to see her hesitate on the steps of the funeral home, hands plunging deep into the pockets of her buttoned coat, her face the color of the old snow banked low beside the sidewalk.

There is the sun rising hard and white from the edges of a pale sky over the quiet screen of trees, the shimmer of ice crystals in the play of light, the whisper of movement in the upper reaches of the trees sifting downward limb to limb, the dry clumps of snow shaken from the low branches as something small darts in the underbrush. There is a hunter, stiff in his thermals and coveralls, peering through his fogged windshield at the tire tracks scarring the surface of the lake. He leaves his truck sputtering just off the rutted road and follows the tracks onto the lake for perhaps two hundred yards, squinting out over the sun blazed ice, shielding his eyes toward a spot a few hundred yards along. He's still studying the dark spot far out on the lake when he tugs his phone from the chest pocket of his coveralls and dials 911 with his thumb. I imagine the car drifting beneath the silent crust of ice, slowly, gracefully, in the thickened water, nose pivoted slightly downward, a few feet above the uneven gray bottom; an unfocused image passing before an occluded eye.

I awaken to the phone call, somewhere around midnight, the line crackling, fading, probably a cell phone. I struggle for my bearings in the well of the bed as a voice asks my name. It asks twice before I manage an answer. The room is warm and dark and Sarah's hand lightly touches my arm. The man on the other end talks for what seems a very long time and I have nothing to say though I manage an occasional affirmation as a means of keeping the conversation from ending. I lean back against the headboard, phone to my ear, closing my eyes for an instant, then opening them again. I click on the bedside lamp and write down the things the officer tells me I should write down. I put the phone down and click off the light, sitting on the side of the bed now, my feet flat upon the floor, my hands upturned in my lap. I remember thinking that my father had finally found the courage to accomplish, in a single act, the one task he'd been beginning again with dedication, day after day, for more than thirty years.

I remember watching as the space emptied behind his eyes, too terrified to turn away, believing I might somehow hold him in place beside me by will alone. Watching as he bled out, leaving his body hollow and animal, leaving a jagged tear in the world, a dark gravity I could never understand which tugged at me nevertheless with the stubborn force of an undertow. He could be at the dinner table or standing at the counter of a convenience store buying a pack of cigarettes. He could be driving the car, his arm hanging over the door, or opening the refrigerator, when the darkness took him and he fell away from me into an annihilating void, his hand sometimes grabbing my arm hard, pulling me toward him, his razored voice snarling in my ear. I remember his darkness burning the world around me and settling onto my chest, whether I pulled away from him or lay in bed in the dark as he careened, stumbling and shouting, through the house; his darkness always more real than the walls separating us.

I imagine a slow grief like an empty house gradually freezing: frost forming on the walls, the plants stiffening in their ceramic pots, water trickling from the faucets in a thin stream, moving slower and slower, sliding along a hardening thread until it stops altogether just above the basin of the sink. The doors and windows crust over, sealing themselves, growing opaque then a lightless blue white. Spider cracks appear in the leather of the sofa and the finish of the dining room table. I imagine a touch like an ice splinter driven deep, melting frigid over time, leaving a wound with no weapon, a cold wound where the flesh cracks and breaks and never heals. I imagine a world sealed within a layer of ice so terribly thin that no-one notices.

She stands before the front door, feet apart, one arm extended, palm spread at the center, as if this simple gesture alone will hold him back. She calls his name, low and soothing, the way one might calm an anxious child. "Lon," she says, "you're not comin' in. Not when you're like this. I don't care where you go, but you're not comin' in." He hammers at the other side, slow and persistent at first, with one hand. I can feel his arm, his cheek, the weight of his body, resting upon the skin of the door and the steady rhythm of the thump thump thump in the darkness of the other side. The screen door leans against his shoulder and squeaks when he shifts position, standing directly before the front door now and hammering hard, shouting "Laauuraa," in a bellow which rolls above the percussion of his fists. I remember the oily heat of the night, the humid sweat of the room. I sit on the couch, fingering the pages of the book in my lap, refusing her pleas to go to bed, my eyes returning again and again to the door and her body erect before it, his blows as steady as a heartbeat tapering slowly to the moist sigh my mother releases when she finally joins me on the couch.

I remember the next morning, staring into the car as I pass on my way to the bus stop. I'm seven years old and the rim of the window falls to eye level. He's asleep in the back seat, lying on his side, hands between his knees. I can smell him through the metal and glass, the sweet thick smell of his drinking and sweat, the car filled with it and the weight of his slurred words. His flannel shirt is twisted around him, his cap lies in the floorboard and there's a thin scar of drool which ends in a puddle on the seat. I shoulder my book bag and hurry past, so my friends waiting on the sidewalk won't be tempted to move toward me or follow my gaze. I meet them at the end of the driveway and we talk about last night's television, my house falling away behind us, and with every breath I silently tell myself, fists knotting at my sides: I will never be like him. Three weeks later he'll drive the car under the back wheels of a transfer truck and spend the next three months in a hospital and I'll visit him there wired into the bed by machines and the fear in his eyes will be limitless and undisguised by alcohol.

I could pitch the photos onto the table, the few that remain, the discarded photos which have never come to rest within an album or a purse. Out of focus, out of frame. Unmarked, undated. I could study them, separately and together. Hunched over the table, knees apart, I could push them across the pale surface, fingering them by their scalloped edges and bent corners, trying to draw forth a date or a history, to conjure a memory which might correspond to the frozen figures before me. I could upend the small box and shuffle the snapshots, experimenting with different arrangements, attempting to construct a story from these random images, attempting to bring an order where one never existed, attempting to discover a beginning and an end to a life which had no direction.

But, these images refuse to create a whole person. Each floats alone and after a time all features blur, the intervening blankness more of a reckoning than the pictures; a cold ghost appearing, not in the captured scenes, but in the space between.

I followed him into the bathroom, talking about school, or a book, or Little League tryouts. We were preparing for an outing together, he and I, an outing which would never materialize because the slights of the world and his own spite would presently become more important. I remember I sat on the edge of the tub, still talking, and he stood before the sink, peeling off his t-shirt, splashing water on his face and chest. He considered himself in the mirror while I studied the scars, random along his back, chest and arms, from fights or falls or not giving a damn. They were ragged tributaries, tangling his body like a net, rising to the surface now and then but most often buried. The scars of a battered skeleton from a forgotten nightmare, they held me at a distance. He was a man who left behind only scars, some old and knotted, others still pink and oozing. His wiry frame housed a rage I inherited like a debt I could not retire. He turned away from the mirror to stare at me, his eyes a blank screen. I stopped talking. The look he gave me told me I was his.

A crack or a boom in the air, which might have been a collision in the parking lot on one side or a muted explosion in the kitchen on the other or something breaking free in the vicinity of my chest. A sound I felt more than heard, around me, a threshold fading into the world. Sarah is bobbing the teabag in her cup, distracted for a moment by the sunlight or a singular swallow bouncing along the sidewalk or my foot nervously dancing upon the opposite knee. I remember my hands flat and angled away from each other on the dark table and the effort with which I kept them still, willing my body to silence while I watched her and listened. I remember the moment she became beautiful, serenely, enduringly beautiful. It wasn't that a new light had entered her face but that I had somehow managed to stumble upon the perspective which revealed her. She bobs her teabag and stares at the sidewalk then raises her eyes to me. She smiles and makes some sort of joke and we both laugh. The revelation of our bruises and histories still to come, one thread at a time. Tears and rage still to come, we sit across the table from each other and laugh.

Now, about the naming of ghosts, the way we name our ghosts, the conditions in which they take shape before us and, finding a witness, we speak; and by speaking we hold the ghost away from its darkness, trap it into vision, trap it until the image drains its power. Now, about this naming of ghosts: drawing them into the room by shout, or by memory, or by turning to meet their blank eyes when their cold hand glances our neck. One ghost after another, or the same over and over, until every seam and wrinkle is committed to memory with the fierce tenderness of a lost love. Now, I stand before Sarah, needing an audience, a witness, not to my pain but to the speaking of it, the organizing of it, the telling of it as a coherent act which retires it somehow like a dog-eared book to a shelf. I tell her of the times his silhouette is more substantial than my own hand but, as I speak, he stumbles in the next room falling against the wall and I hear the lamp break from my bedroom and my mother's voice and there seems to be no way to release it. Sarah before me, we stand séance-like, hands clasped facing each other, or lie abed in the dark, or stare out a flickering car window. We draw our ghosts down upon us by virtue of the spark between us, feeling the pull of our dark litanies yet turning toward each other nonetheless. We begrudgingly accept the terror of grace.

I remember his taut arms around my eight year old shoulders, his calloused hands closing over mine and the bat, bringing it back and leading it out low and even at my side. They were firm and confident, encircling me, drawing me close. The tang of his aftershave and the sandy stubble of his cheek. I could feel the fluid grace of his swing and the joy of solid contact with the ball in his bones. One day, one summer, one afternoon for an hour or two, when he tossed it slow and I stood feet apart, the way he'd taught me, swinging. He threw and I swung, running to collect the ball in the backyard, quick and awkward so as not to lose a moment, and tossing it back so he could throw again, again and again, until I found the tone of my swing, the ball startling the bat and sailing over his head. Enjoying the ache in my fingers, the thud of contact, and his smile as he watched it float past, feeling a pleasure in the moment which haunts me still.

It makes it harder for her to speak, so I don't look. I don't hold her. I stare up into the darkness, her lips near my ear. We're thrown across the bed, on our backs atop the crisp sheet. I gaze into the darkness as Sarah speaks, my awareness resting at the threshold of her voice. There's a damp heat upon our skin and a slight breeze filling the room from the open window. I can hear the curtain rustling against the frame. She speaks of what she carries, fashioning the past from dream or memory, shaping the weight of it and the shadows left upon her skin, the thin patterns of loss, the surges of fear. Tears previously shed are condensed now to a single teardrop which slides across the bridge of her nose and falls to the pillow. She speaks slowly, her voice even, the sentences broken only by protracted phrases of silence in which her breath is all that is audible, deep and measured. At one point she turns onto her side, facing me, arms folded over her chest, edging closer until her lips are nearly touching my ear and she whispers her tender secrets so gently that it takes all of my concentration simply to follow the words.

The way my fist shot out toward the wall of its own accord. The gratifying thud and the crumbling of sheetrock. The impact backing up my arm and into my shoulders, awakening some sleeping musculature beneath my skin. Needing a hard edge, a sharp edge, my wiry skeleton unfolding bitter within me and needing impact at bone at skin, the dense press of the world at my throat to match the pace of my breath. Needing a target. The book leaving my hand where I stand, sailing by Sarah and striking the wall where it punches a hole and falls to the floor. Sarah's head turning slowly from the book to me, her eyes wrestling equal parts anger and fear, her eyes fixing me within her gaze. And I am whirring inside a fully-breathed rage which has no story. Needing to move, needing to run. Afraid of myself. Needing to leave. I've got to go, I tell her. Her eyes do not leave me. The way her arm extends where she stands, her hand flattening softly upon the skin of the front door. "No," she says, "I think you should stay." And I believe her.

I imagine the scene as if I'm standing directly behind the car, the exhaust fading in the cold before it reaches me. Through the back windshield, the silhouette of his head in the green-glow of the dashboard dials and the slant of the headlights before him. The edge of the unshaven chin, the bill of the cap, the amber of the cigarette dangling from his lips, glowing and receding with his breath. There is no shift within his body once the decision is made, no indication of its certainty. He leans to the right, resting an elbow on the middle console and his attitude doesn't change when he punches the accelerator and tunnels away from me into the night. The headlights swing left from the muffled trees. The tires spin at first then catch in the powdery snow, jerking the car onto the lake. He moves out into the darkness, toward the center. In a moment, all I can see is the hot glow of the taillights growing smaller. And soon, he's swallowed by the night, the cold, the ice, into a stillness like the falling of paper.

I remember standing in the snow for a long time, my feet growing cold in my dress shoes, my socks wet where slush had crept under my cuffs, unsure of what I was waiting for, unsure of what I wanted, studying the blank façade of the funeral home, its three stone steps and empty windows, my eyes shifting side to side, restless, then inching upward to the roof, to the chimney, to the white plume bleeding into the cold white of the sky, the thick smoke billowing forth like the sheet Sarah and I unfurl over the bare mattress, she on one side of the bed and I on the other, each corner held taut between us as we lower it over the bed and I tuck my side under, smoothing the creases while she tucks her side and we brush at the sheet, she on her side and me on mine, flattening it until it spills between us with the promise of a blank page awaiting the first touch of ink to give it life.

From the deck I can make out faint threads of the tide as they dissolve along the shore. The darkness is even and cool, the sand releasing the heat of the day to the breeze. Faraway boats flicker at an invisible horizon. The door slides open behind me and Sarah's scent precedes her as she steps toward her chair. She leans back, her slender fingers tracing the length of my bare arm to grasp my thumb and draw my hand to rest upon her belly, rounded softly beneath her t-shirt and still warm with the memory of sun. The tide mutters somewhere in the darkness. I remember the tilt of her head this morning at the breakfast table, the mischievous shift of her smile, her eyes canting toward me in some mundane and spontaneous burst of discovery, as if, once again, she were seeing me for the first time. I imagine my fingers gently caressing a scar along her inner thigh, night after night, until one morning we find it has vanished. I imagine her hand drifting across the table, over napkins and silver and the crumbs of the meal, to rest warm upon mine.

I imagine the jolt as the frigid water snarls around him, the sharp intake of breath. I imagine the boom as the ice splinters, his hands closing tight around the wheel as he gasps. The front wheels buoyed for an instant, the rear wheels hanging at the crust of ice before it gives way. The car easing into the water, exhaling slowly front to back, drifting beneath the surface, the rear bumper scraping the underside of the ice as the current claims it. The darkness is total, the lights blinking out in the dark green water just before his first liquid breath. His eyes are open, his jaw growing slack. I imagine when they finally pulled him from the river many hours later, blue cold and stiff, fifty yards downstream from the jagged hole in the ice; I imagine then that they wrapped his dripping body in a clean sheet, winding it around his form as if swaddling an infant. I imagine that to be the most intimate contact afforded him in years and years.

Vertigo Run

I perform my nightly surrender, different this time because I am hurtling through space and surrounded by strangers. I forget the meetings of the previous days and the anxiety over whether Michaelson will sign, I forget the reports due Monday. Folding my laptop and sliding it into the case at my feet, I float toward a stillness, the kind of glassy Zen pool I had heard about once at a workshop, the kind with Japanese flute music and discreet waterfalls, the kind that worries my boss whenever I make the mistake of mentioning it.

When I open my eyes, it is late and the cabin is warm, most of the lights dimmed or off, the ambient engine hum broken sporadically by the sudden rustle of the air conditioning. I am nestled within the arms of my travel family, relieved of artifice since I will never see them again. A woman behind me whispers with her husband about their daughter's appalling taste in clothes and boys, the man beside me rattles papers across the shell of his computer; I can hear the distant murmur of someone's iPod a few rows up.

I drift, allowing the plane to lose detail, allowing my

mind to settle into the syllables of the unseen woman. I might be curling into the seat; I might be six years old and folding into a corner of the sofa as loose-limbed as a kitten, dodging sleep, while my parents and the other adults talk, laugh; my mother's hand drifting toward me now and then to absently touch my hair or caress my ankle. It feels safe to be nearly asleep in a room with others, at the fringe of conversations I don't understand and don't want to understand. The comfort of their speaking permits me to fade; I can trust that someone is awake to hold the world in place in my absence.

The boundaries of solid objects have always seemed less sure at night. If I am still, I can believe they are transparent, ghostly, and it is only when I move that they shudder to definition as if frightened to a single stance. Drowsing on the plane, objects fade and return, percolating from solid to liquid to gas while remaining, somehow, essential.

It's two in the morning by the time we land and the terminal is abandoned, the arrival board hopefully blinking detailed information to no-one. The pulse of the night slows even more perceptibly in our ragged shuffle through the boarding gate. We shamble into the concourse as a body, then break into individual corpuscles after baggage claim, each moving with our own logic.

I climb into an idling cab, my mind rousing my body to a semblance of consciousness. The driver nods somnambulantly at my address, nosing the car left and into the road. I consider the requisite conversation but decide against it and he doesn't appear offended. His eyes study me in the rear view mirror for three seconds of habitual curiosity then lock to the road and never stray. I settle in the seat, allowing my body to fill the crevices of the worn upholstery, blinking at the oily smear of neon on the road before us.

Something in the silence, underscored by the brush of the tires upon the road beneath us, reminds me of Erica, of our hiking trip years ago, of splashing wine into plastic cups balanced upon a rock, of following a thin stream of spilled wine as it edges toward the cliff and our patient anticipation, cups in hand, as we wait to toast the first drop to fall.

Something in the silence is dangerous, fluttering stomach twitching hands dangerous, dangerous with a gasp and a thrill; as dangerous as the day on the mountain when the altitude and the wine and the exertion combined to catalyze a language and we began to talk with each other as if we had always known and we stayed on the cliff, refilling our glasses, until nearly dark and had to struggle down the path, hand to outstretched hand, stumbling into the heat and darkness of the trees, toward the only car left in the lot.

As the car snaked around the mountain she slid closer, pretending it was gravity, centrifugal force, and by the base our hands found each other again, quietly, as innocent as cats, and our language remained. I relaxed into the seat then, as I do now; I watched the night with calm while always aware of its churning mystery, as if the next turn might find us in another county or an undiscovered past.

This slipping connection with memory, once made, establishes a circuit, allows the possibility of memory as a place, an address. The cab driver's hands slide along the rim of the wheel in the turn, both our bodies tilting left in our seats, as synchronous as birds on a line. I am convinced he is humming quietly to himself, yet when I concentrate, attempting to focus on the melody, it darts away, his hum apparently operating at a frequency I cannot hear when attentive.

The road is nearly empty, the darkness deepening, as we pass the shopping centers and convenience stores signaling civilization. I am meandering home while his travels are the random trajectory of an insect, alighting first upon one stem then another. We drift, sharing our capsule, the planet falling away on either side of the road, the brightly lit buildings forming a simple boundary separating order from the unknown.

The taxi washes into my driveway and hushes to a stop, the driver simply motioning with a slight smile, not bothering to speak, as I hand him the folded bills. He doesn't count them either, trusting me perhaps from the core of our shared silence; or simply tired, wanting to be alone, wanting the open road instead of wordless companionship. He manages an absent wave as he turns, throwing an arm atop the bench seat, to back into the street.

I let myself in. The kitchen tumbles into place beneath my gaze. The refrigerator takes its position in the corner, the windows align to my left and the floor flows gently over the threshold and out, into the dining room. I don't turn on the light. I slide the suitcase low around the plane of the door and slip the carry-on from my shoulder.

I click the door closed and the dry rattle of the trees disappears behind it. I stand motionless, hands loose at my sides, patiently affording a chance for the night to collect around me, to spin from the forward tilt of the last hours, the last days, to cycle down and come to rest within the house and within me, my organs gradually matching its tone until we inhabit the room together.

I plant my first step upon solid ground. I reach out, resting my hand upon the granite counter by the sink, pushing off from there toward the dark threshold, penetrating the house with stealth, testing its permanence in my absence: the dining room table and its fan of mail; the shoes resting beside the sofa, one upright, the other on its side; the photos along the mantle soldiering in discrete angles, one year behind the next, resting, yet attentive.

I slip from my jacket and fold it over the arm of the sofa, pushing from my shoes and deserting them by the others on the floor. I remember myself into the room, the location seeping back into me, the house molding me into the form which had lost definition in travel. I pad into the darkened hallway deliberately, brushing my fingers along the wall on both sides, a child discovering the fresh reach of his growing arms; the wall rough and cool at my knuckles, the carpet thick beneath my socks.

I am four or five, resting atop my father's wide shoulders and we are moving through a huge crowd, angling our way around clumps of spectators, penetrating occasional openings in the group, jockeying for the best position in which to watch a parade. I am shocked, open-mouthed, at my panoramic view of the world above everyone's head. It is a thrill discovered whole in the world. I bounce within his stride.

My hands are clasped to Dad's forehead and every now and then I slip them down tightly over his eyes and he does not hesitate, but smiles. I guide him through the crowd by turning his head, I steer him around an entire family, I slow him by pulling back, giggling all the time, his shoulders beneath me spasming in laughter.

And when I pull him to a halt at the precise location I have chosen, I allow the blindfold of my fingers to slip away and he grins happily at where we have arrived, flexing his eyes up toward me, patting his broad hands upon my shins in approval.

The heat of her sleep fills the room. I pause before the open bedroom door, lingering at the edge, attempting to take in its fullness without impressing myself. The faint blue glow of the alarm clock rises up the far wall, fading into the slatted shadow thrown by the streetlight through the blinds. The scents are so familiar as to be invisible, save the hint of a new perfume, having faded with the day to mere suggestion. I cannot hear her breathing from the doorway but, in a moment: the slide of a bare foot between the sheets and the hiss as it comes to rest.

I hold the image as if inventing it. I shape the room around her sleeping form in the same care as she holds the house in place in my absence. I trust, when I return, that room will follow room and she will be curled into the sofa or burrowed deep into the bed or sipping coffee by the window, as she believes that my waking glance, or the heat of my skin against her, or the pulse of our ongoing years, will tether her to place within the grace of her abandonment.

There is something dangerous in this darkness, fluttering stomach twitching hands dangerous, dangerous with a gasp and a thrill. The doorway threatens to burn away all protection and release me into an order I cannot understand or even bear. It is a frenzy simultaneous with an absolute stillness, a voltage less adrenalin than rippling, more akin to the fragile movement of light in the interval between the future and dream.

I move toward the bed, standing at the side, absently unbuttoning my shirt while staring down to my feet, steady upon the floor. I balance upon one leg, then another, peeling off my socks and tossing them into the corner with my shirt. Erica's face, lost in sleep, turns toward me with the startle of a clean, full moon.

I am in a stairwell, pressure and force around me; I am ten or twelve or fourteen. I am tearing down the stairs as fast as possible. Faster. My legs pressing hard enough that my feet barely keep pace: a place somewhere between running and flight, between flight and collapse.

I am plummeting at the brink of disaster, my legs frantic to support my racing body, already leaning forward, pressing downward, no longer aware of each step as it comes, only of the fine, unbroken line which I follow from the last step to the next landing, the clean, unbroken wave bearing me forward, the thread which keeps my body upright.

Several boys are running with me; we tumble as a group, a stampede of shouts and shrieks, all of us encouraging the others, supporting the others, all of us throwing ourselves into trust with equal speed, the window at the landing hurtling by before the next descent down and around five flights, thundering as a juddering body, stair to landing to stair, to burst through the heavy schoolhouse doors swinging wide and banging hard into the brick behind us, exploding into the autumn courtyard, our lungs aching, our legs rubbery, collapsing into each other in a sweat and a pant and losing our footing at last in the sodden carpet of leaves.

I won't wake her. I'll undress, dropping the remainder of my stale clothes to the floor by the bedside table and placing my watch near the alarm clock. I'll draw the blankets back gently and drift into the open fold beside her. I won't touch her, afraid that I might wake her. Instead, I will lie still, falling into my skin beside her.

And, in the morning she will be the first to draw

herself from our envelope of sleep and, in my dream I will feel her leaning on her elbow by my side and my eyelids will flutter, struggling with the oblique morning light to make out her face, and it is then that she will lean toward me, resting her hand open upon my chest, and kiss me and our day will begin.

Home

S he opens her eyes.
  She'd squeezed them closed, waiting for the voices to pass her by. As if closing them might allow her to disappear. It was a ritual she'd believed in when she was younger, but now she's nearly eleven and has lost her faith.

She's wedged between the chest freezer and the cinder block wall of the basement in her own house. The block cool at her back. The freezer's compressor oozing a syrupy warmth into her face. It clicks on and off at irregular intervals, the motor rattling to life. Startling her each time.

There's barely room to breathe. Her knees pressed to the rear of the machine, chest pressed to her knees, back to the wall. Grime and furred dust coats the floor beneath her, sticky on the skin. Clumping to her hands as she pushes further into the corner. Her heartbeat skitters along her damp and gritty palms. She tilts her head upward toward the open air. She can't hear anyone moving now.

But she doesn't trust the silence. She decides, even with her heart shuddering, to wait.

And in a moment, footsteps, attempting quiet. They pad to the front of the freezer, stop, then move further into the depths of the basement. They shift boxes along a near wall, scudding them out along the floor. There are whispers.

The cardboard scrapes roughly over the cement, first in one direction then the other. The footsteps move to a far wall. She hears murmuring, someone calling. It might be her name. She curls her toes in her sneakers, tenses her palms into the block at her back.

She had learned to cope with fear. When she was younger and she lay in her bed. Her father had allowed her to sleep with the light on for quite a while but, finally one night, he'd turned the light off and lay in the bed beside her.

He'd spoken softly, guiding her to trace her breathing until it slowed. To feel the blanket warm upon her skin, the bed solid beneath her, the doll soft in her hand. To find a center. At first, it had been impossible to follow his voice but then, something in the timbre and constancy of it allowed her shoulders to ease and then her mind to follow his suggestions without the delay of thinking. Until she'd fallen asleep.

He'd done this for three successive nights. Lying on the bed beside her, most of his body overhanging the narrow mattress. His lips near her ear, his arm at her side. Close, but not touching. He'd led her away from her fear and into her body.

On the fourth night, after he'd said goodnight, he switched off the light and shut the door. She'd pressed her eyes closed and felt calmed. But the fear was familiar. It had a taste she could roll on her tongue there in the dark. Testing it, savoring it.

The fear was erratic. Abandoning her for days or weeks then returning in an instant. It was familiar enough that at times she longed for it. At times she smiled in the moments of its first touch, before its full terror overtook her.

As soon as she'd been old enough to recognize it, she'd lain rigid in horror. Or screamed. And her father would come, turn on the light and comfort her back to sleep. After a while, he allowed her to sleep with the light on.

What happened when she opened her eyes, then and now on the fourth night, was this. The walls of her room began to waver, first in the corners and just on the edge of her vision. She saw them as something liquid. As she watched, the walls lost their shape around her. Then she began to see through them. Not into the hallway or the room bordering her own. Into another place. She peered through one life and into the fine structures of another.

And then she would scream. And her father would come. But not on the fourth night. On the fourth night, she floated upon her leveling breath. The well of the bed beneath her. The lingering scent of her Dad.

The walls began to shimmer. She watched the room around her shift, growing larger, more spacious. The veil of the world slipped. She felt she could begin to see all of the shadow forces and they weren't there to harm her. She was still frightened. But she could watch without screaming.

The space behind the freezer grows tighter. She waits, whispering softly to herself to keep from moving, to keep from pushing herself toward the opening or crying out. She scrapes the back of her hand along the block for the pain of it, the jagged sensation rising into her arm.

Maybe twenty feet away: the thunder of running and shouts. She turns her head toward the opening and peers into the darkened slit of the room. They'd found Abigail. She hears the screams, off to the left near the basement stairs. She hears them struggle.

A fine thread of fear spins into her stomach. Angular and icy. Tingling to the tips of her fingers. Calming her somehow. Exciting her.

She closes her eyes. She is no longer folded within the space behind the freezer. It might as well have vanished. She's imagining, now, the chalk circle in the center of the basement floor which is home. She can't see it. She feels it in her chest and her stomach, a new warmth within the thrill and terror.

Abigail is laughing now. And Alex and Ben. They'd already caught Lucy and Bill. And Sandy. Mariel is the last one.

She opens her eyes. I know she opens her eyes. The wall presses against my body, the damp-earth scent of the basement fills my nostrils.

The sky is gray outside the window and I'm nearly naked in the cold. Flushed and damp. I can feel the wind whipping up through the rough floor of the meditation hut to catch at my skin. I can feel the wind, I can see the window. But I'm crouched behind the freezer, the block cool at my scraped knuckles. That's where I'm present. Picturing the chalk boundary etched upon the basement floor.

I scrape my knuckles against the block until the skin curls off in fine strands. I squint toward the narrow opening between freezer and block into the darkness of the basement.

"Are you cold, Mariel?" Will asks me from the floor. His fingers stroke the top of my hand, flat upon the boards. My elbow holding me upright and close to the window. His skin is warm against mine and I feel the weight of his body behind the caress. "A little," I tell him.

"Why don't you come down here."

"I'm fine. I like the window right now."

"Sometimes," he confesses, not for the first time, "you really confuse me."

I turn to him, away from the window of the hut, away from the block wall and the basement. He's lying askew upon the rough floor. His shirt unbuttoned and twisted around him, his pants at his ankles. His eyes are blue and clear and he's watching me because it's something he likes to do.

"Do you want a world without mystery?" I ask him. And he laughs.

His laugh changes the space around me for a moment. I feel it close and taut along my skin. And for just a moment I consider that I could stay and the entire world might focus into a single shape and he would hold me.

His laugh changes the way I think for a moment. I consider arranging my furniture around it into the shape of a nice warm room at the center of an inviting house. I could choose the wallpaper and the curtains to match the texture of his laugh. I could find the colors to mimic the quality of his caress.

His laugh is a different place to settle. Like a stone at the bottom of a fast moving stream. A location I might share, resting until the final closing of my eyes. His laugh is a surprise, a door bursting open in a gust of wind.

Or the flush of my first meeting with Antonia Beck. It had been here in the meditation hut, but it had been spring then, two years ago, and the air was heavy and green. My decision to move to a spiritual community, to Monmouth in particular, had been a strategy for upending my life, for completing a first draft and beginning the second with a flourish. I expected it to draw me further into myself in a complex series of exchanges with invisible beings, but the apocalypse, when it comes, is always simple. And quiet.

It's a shift in the light. Nothing more.

I'd read Antonia Beck's books; I was sincerely drawn to her teaching and the idea of devoting myself to a spiritual practice. I imagined it to be an anonymous and unassuming enterprise, so I was nervous when I met her. I was sent, like every Prospective, down a winding path through the trees to arrive at the small raised hut in the center of a wide circular wall of stacked stones. I was reminded of Hansel and Gretel.

But, once inside the Meditation Hut, there was no hungry witch, only Antonia, seated on a cushion near a window, waiting for me. I babbled and she was quiet. She must have spoken that day but I can't remember a word. I remember her stillness. Her patience. Her eyes. It wasn't what I expected.

I expected to work in the gardens, with the animals. I expected to hum God's frequency. I imagined myself melting away. I counted on a form of silence and hoped for a revelation which might order the whole of the cosmos around me. I was merely following my frontier strategy of devising safe locations within the light, then moving away again, into a deeper darkness. Focusing my center down to a dense, golden star.

I never imagined Antonia and I would simply become friends, not teacher and supplicating student, but friends who talked about movies and language and the embarrassments of our own humanity. I never imagined we would take up residence within each other, readily, hungrily.

When Antonia abandoned Monmouth nine months later without a word to anyone, I understood. I found her note pinned to my screen door early that morning. The rest is up to you, it said. And that's all it said.

I'd initiated this relationship with Will from the vacant ache of Antonia's absence. From an urgency which spasmed through my lower body, rising then into my face in a heavy steam. I'd wanted a lever to wrench me from my stable orbit at Monmouth and hurtle me outward into the void. This need had drawn me toward him, pushed me to speak, and laid me open all at once.

But I had nothing to talk to him about. Nothing to tell him.

I watch him sometimes, when he's working with the animals or reading in his room. He seems easy with his secrets. Delicate and watchful. He moves as if he has nothing to hide. I watch him now, sprawled on the floor around me, his eyes on my face, my breast, my hand. He touches me as if he knows me, but he doesn't.

Antonia knows me. She simply saw me. Fully. And the reflection was enough to burn the image deep into bone.

I blink and I can see us, sitting in the back yard of her house. Barefoot in the damp grass even in the rain. The dark bowl of the sky above us. We sat in old lawn chairs, twirling bottles of Rolling Rock between our fingers by the neck. We talked, over the course of a summer and a fall. About everything. As if we were inventing and naming a world.

It wasn't a string of revelations between us. It was a silence and an occasional glance. It was in the way we watched the night around us, noticing every rustle in the grass and balancing star. Never pointing these things out. Assuming the other was listening, watching, just as intently.

It was a way of talking which built worlds and thoughts and feelings while the grass cooled and dampened between our toes. It was something we made together which burned above us, just outside our reach.

The field before us would be wide and dark, the oaks

and locusts rising as shadows acres away. There were no houses close by and the nearest city was sixty miles. In the summer, the staccato rhythms of the fireflies. In the fall, the low rumble and crash of the cows and the quickening rattle of the leaves. Antonia would sometimes sit with her head thrown back along the aluminum rim of her lawn chair. One hand open on the plastic armrest, the other dangling her bottle above the grass.

I betrayed the rest of the world with Antonia Beck. Betrayed everything we agree the world to be. Every rule of logic and physics, every shared ethic.

I betrayed my past. I surrendered fragments of a future. I could see myself doing it; I turned each one between my fingers then let them go. I gave up a certain vision of myself. I gave it all over to a crystalline loneliness.

On those nights, we re-imagined each other. Simply by talking far into ourselves. It was a tacit agreement, never spoken. We touched only occasionally, accidentally. We shaped our world. On those nights I visited places I couldn't easily return from. On those nights, Antonia released me into doubt and I freed her, somehow, from Monmouth.

And in the morning, in the light and shuffle of the day, we held our secrets close, tender against our skin. As if we were sheltering a fragile creature, a wet butterfly, a frightened bird. In the mornings, we smiled our secrets between us; each with our own work, each in our own world.

There's so much I can't tell Will, so much I don't talk about. There is one thing I could say but I don't. I could say: I know the imprint of touch, I know the mark it leaves.

The window is still there. The window has not

changed. Nor has the gray screen of the low sky. Will strokes my hand and I let him, my eyes on the distance, goose bumps rising along my arms.

He draws me down toward him. My cool breasts resting upon his cool chest until a warmth begins to form again between us. I kiss him. We make love again. My body gasps in the motion and joy of it. I'm happy to be with him. Happy to be making love, to be warm where our skins meet and cool where the winter air brushes me.

Later, we dress. Standing up, tugging our limbs into our clothes. Facing each other. Shuddering in the cold, now that our bodies have separated. Staring at each other until we laugh.

Seated outside on the wooden steps, I pull on my sneakers. It's deep fall and the leaves have filled the raked space around the hut. The low surrounding rock wall holds them in rattling pools. The cows have already passed. Entering their winter lethargy early, they've meandered toward the far side of the property, one following the other.

Will is straightening cushions inside. I can hear him through the open door at my back. He pulls the door closed and stands on the top step behind me. The wind begins to pick up as the light fails, the cold seeps up from the earth. He descends the stairs past me. He stands at the bottom, looking up.

I scrape the back of my hand along the rough step beneath me, the grain of the wood rasping into my fingers and arm. She scrapes her hand along the coarse block beside her. She is turned now in the opening between the freezer and the wall. Turned into the open darkness of the basement.

He draws me toward him to stand. He straightens my bomber jacket around me and zips it up. He takes

my reddened hand and kisses the knuckles. He doesn't
let my hand go.

We walk away from the hut, our secrets tender and
untold between us. An alternate history we do not
address. We hold hands until we reach the wall. Like
teenagers in the parking lot of the spring dance, unsure
whether to be proud or embarrassed.

On the fourth night, Mariel had lain in her bed and
the walls had dissolved and the bed had floated free
and her body had burned off and the world had spun a
whirlwind around her. Before, she had always screamed
for her Dad.

Now she could find his voice within her, winding its
way around a tiny pinprick of light. A light which did
not move, but shimmered and burned bright. She felt
him close. Closer even than he had been, lying upon
the bed beside her.

The frame of the room fell away into the darkness
and she did not scream, though her breath caught in
her throat and her pulse doubled. Before, this change
had always terrified her but now it seemed beautiful.
Solid and true. Not a nightmare at all.

They're all looking for her. Stationed throughout the
clutter of the basement. They're all calling her name from
different locations. But she only has to avoid Alex and Ben.

She would scramble from behind the freezer, make
the six feet to the corner wall, then turn left. The chalk
circle would be twenty feet straight ahead. The basement
was crowded with boxes and junk. She'd have to ease
past the garden equipment and appliances. Once she
made the turn, she'd have to watch the stairs. They were
dangerously close to the circle and Alex or Ben might
be hiding there.

Her hands cupped upon the concrete floor, she draws
herself to her knees behind the freezer. Her limbs unfold

into the open darkness. Her knees are stiff from the cramped space and tremble as she stands. She grasps the edge of the freezer to steady herself.

Sandy is calling her name close and to the right, laughing as she calls. Mariel slides toward the corner wall, more stable now. Her eyes flicker over the room in the near dark, articulating shadows.

She eases past an old lawnmower, close to the wall, without falling over it. Tennis rackets hang from the ceiling. A garden hose is coiled high at her side. Sandy is coming up close to her right, her voice growing nearer. Mariel peers toward Sandy's voice, hoping to judge the distance.

Alex rounds the corner, five feet away, Sandy at his side. He stares blankly at Mariel for an instant. Their eyes meet and his face lights into a grin.

She bursts from the corner and into the long stretch toward the circle. The area is open, appliances and bicycles lining the walls. She can see Abigail standing near the circle, her back turned, watching the stairs to the right.

"She's here!" Alex shouts, at her heels, "I've got her!"

Abigail turns, her hands coming up before her in surprise. When she sees Mariel, she leaps into the air. Laughing, clapping her hands, cheering her forward.

Her body arches in a surge, her legs bearing her forward and up. Her breath is hot and hard against her teeth. Her legs extend to their full length. The basement, the house, vanishes. She can hear the voices rising around her. The rustle and pant of Alex at her back. There's only the distance between her and the circle.

She laughs in the exhilaration, the release. Her body taking a new shape. Her breath emptying her lungs and thrusting her forward. Alex galloping behind, his arm extended to tag her. Abigail clapping near the stairs. Ben descending the steps in a panic, knowing he's too late.

The leaves crunch and scatter beneath our feet and we don't say a word, even when we reach the stone wall. Reflexively, Will's hand slides from mine as he steps over. For some reason, I stop.

I hear Will turn back to me from the other side of the wall. I hadn't realized my eyes were closed until the sound of him. I open my eyes. I raise them to him. Then he knows I'm leaving. And I know he's staying.

She tears through the basement. The old toys and broken bicycles, the washer and dryer, blurring past. The other kids are all laughing now, cheering dramatically. It's come down to just her and Alex.

Her lungs are bursting, her legs ache. Alex's breath is close at her back. She can sense his hand near. He grabs her shirt, spinning her around. Sweating, laughing. Running past her, unable to stop. But she's already inside the circle.

I step over the wall into the border of trees, blinking into the light between branches. I step away from a place I knew as a child. A place my father helped me to discover. A place I lose and find. Again and again.

Platform

We didn't know each other before April 9. Most of us had never met. We might have nodded, occasionally and in passing, to one another on the platform now and then. But we didn't know each other. We were simply traveling together.

All of us waited on the platform, patiently or nervously. Pacing and looking at our watch or quietly reading our paper. Easing toward work or school or, later, maybe a date and dinner. All of us moving in different directions, the way we all do.

And when the train hissed to a stop, we lined ourselves before the doors and, when the doors slid open, we lined ourselves into the cars. Spreading into the seats, the corners, standing in the aisles. Waiting collectively for the doors to close and the train to jump to a start.

But we didn't know each other. If we ever looked at each other it was an accident of will. We might smile and immediately glance away or we might not smile, an expression being too articulate an acknowledgement of the other person.

April 9 was different. On April 9, fifteen minutes into our journey, five minutes before the fourth stop, the lights went out in the cars and the train slowed to a halt in the tunnel. The overheads blinked off, leaving us with only the steel blue emergency lights glowing at the floor.

This was after the coughing began at the front of the car. After the first man fell there and the Oriental woman began clutching her throat. We heard the brakes grab hold beneath us, heard their rasp and felt it at our feet through the floor as they closed around the tracks.

Some of us were already moving toward the front of the car. A woman screamed and a child began to cry when the lights flickered and the brakes shuddered. The man at the front fell to the floor and someone bent toward him as he began to convulse.

We became one then, for a moment. All of us there in the car. We moved separately as conjoined limbs of the same body. Even the young boy who cowered beneath his seat and the older woman who covered her face with her hands and emitted a low wail. Even they were a part of that singular body; each individual performing their own mysterious and essential function.

It was dark, with only the blue of the emergency lights reflecting shadows from the dead windows. Feet scraped against the metal floor. The man at the front began to gurgle and a number of others near him began to cough. The Oriental woman fell to the floor atop her grocery bag. Someone threw themselves at the metal door on the right side of the car.

I was standing along the back wall, my hands in my coat pockets. I was watching the first man to fall. He was bleeding from the nose and mouth. I could see the blood when the blue emergency lights blinked on at the floor. It looked black, dripping from his nose to the corrugated metal. His eyes were wide at first. He drew his legs to his chest, his arms twitching before him as his body closed around itself.

There was something in my chest that felt like waiting. Simmering there against the back wall of the car. It slipped from my chest to tingle in the tips of my fingers. I watched the movements of the others. I heard the sounds of coughing and gasping, the sounds of dying.

The air of the car was liquid, it ebbed against the skin of my face. I slid down the wall of the car in the blue light, my legs folding beneath me, until I stopped. I drew my hands from my coat pockets. I placed my hands, palms down, upon the cold metal floor.

We didn't know each other. I tried explaining that to the burly paramedic who was standing near me, checking on those still alive. We were on the platform by then. We were sitting along the rough benches, huddled in blankets with bottles of water. We were trying not to look at the bodies lined further down the concourse, haphazardly covered in plastic sheeting.

I tried to push past the questions about this man or that child or who had brought the bag into the car and explain that we didn't know each other but it didn't seem to matter. What I said. It didn't seem to make any difference. I wanted to find something hopeful to say. About our anonymity, our humanity. I wanted to be hopeful with those around me. I wanted to say that pain was essential to change. I wanted to tell a story.

About perseverance. And transformation. My story, but I would change it a bit to make it more universal. Less personal.

And I told that story at the ER. To the lady in the seat beside me, listening inattentively. It was important to tell it. To someone. You see, I know I've been changed.

In the last two years. In the last days, in the last few

hours. I am not the same person that I was. I see the world differently and it is that difference which I wanted to pass along. Explain. To someone. Maybe it had something to do with the proximity of death.

So, I talked in the waiting room of the ER. To no-one in particular. To the lady beside me. Something simply opened up inside in a way I hadn't felt in years. And I talked. About that morning, about my job and the Nova project. About Janet. I talked a lot about Janet.

If not for Janet leaving, I would not be where I was. I wouldn't be living in the city, wouldn't have the new job. If not for Janet leaving, I would never have met Mother and the others of the Church. I would not have been changed.

I talked for a moment in the ER about how I felt the morning I knew she was gone. I didn't go into the argument or the night before. I wanted to focus clearly on that single moment and the realization that I was absolutely alone. The terror, the exhilaration of it. The cold light at the windows.

The ER was crowded and noisy. It was difficult to tell how many people were ranged along the walls and on the floor. We had all been transported by bus. They wanted to examine everyone. Figure out what had happened. The police and the paramedics, they didn't want anyone to go home from the platform until they had been seen.

Soon after we were unloaded from the bus, a large police trailer drew up in the parking lot outside the building and we could see, through the windows, as the officers stepped out of the trailer onto the asphalt. They began taking us in, two at a time, for interviews.

Some of us were still crying. Many of the children had fallen asleep in tears on their parents' lap. Interns and nurses moved amongst the crowd, handing out more bottles of water and occasionally tapping an ill passenger on the shoulder then leading them through the double doors to an examining room.

The lady beside me cried softly, her cheeks damp and swollen with tears, her eyes red-rimmed and puffy. She muttered under her breath as I spoke, rocking slightly, forward and back. I hoped that my story might somehow calm her.

Of course, the conversation naturally turned to Mother and the Church. I needed to start with the morning Janet left, the morning I found myself alone, to give the necessary context. I needed to tell her about the moment I discovered my life was false. The morning two years ago, when I had glanced out the kitchen window. The ground had been dry and cold, the trees bare. A squirrel had darted in one direction then another, following some unseen directive, then it had clambered up a tree.

I described the moment to her completely because, even now, I remember it completely. It continues to bloom, that specific event, throughout every moment of my life. I looked out the window and knew that everything I believed was a lie. Janet's note on the refrigerator didn't bring this about. It was simply the last vestige of the illusion. Gone.

"Oh, Lord," muttered the lady next to me. She drew her beige corduroy coat tighter around her neck with a clenched hand, "Oh, Lord. Help me."

She wasn't looking at anyone. She wasn't speaking to anyone. She was rocking, staring at the floor before her. There was a cut on her forehead, above her right eye, and blood had dried there.

I quit my job. After Janet left. Moved to the city. A new job in a larger firm and a one bedroom apartment. I didn't stay there much. I walked a lot. All hours of the night, block after block, in graduating circles around my apartment and back again. I wasn't looking for anything in particular. I walked simply to be going somewhere.

I walked past storefronts, with shoppers. And parks with children. I walked past cars and traffic. Day and night. I began to see the world differently, the world outside of myself. Every time I closed the apartment door behind me and stepped out into the street, I felt smaller, more nameless.

Before that, I had always been the center of the universe. The planets had spun around me. As I walked, the world grew larger and my own part in it grew smaller. Until it hardly existed. I began to see the necessity for change, the necessity for something radical.

One night, I walked off the edge of the world and I fell. I lost my foothold and I fell. I continued to fall, the city sliding past me in strobing muted colors, passersby calling my name. And when the falling slowed for a moment, when my limbs flailed outward for something solid, I found myself in Mother's arms.

I was drawn by the singing, by joy. It rolled from the open storefront doors onto the sidewalk and streets in a warming wave and my body responded while my mind was still searching for its origin. There was something in the voices and the way they melded together. Not in perfect harmony. Nothing like that. In something much more motley, beautiful and human.

Mother met me at the threshold as if she already knew my name, as if we were old friends. Clasping both of her hands around my own and holding me to the spot. As if I were in danger of spinning away from her in the waves of singing. And maybe I was.

She held me tight within both of her hands and bored deep into my eyes with her solitary stare and for the first time in months, perhaps years, I didn't mind being seen. "Welcome," she said. Those are my memories of that night. The singing, the warm summer air. Mother's hands around mine and the single word.

After that night, I fell in a different way. Lighter, gentler. It was less like falling, more like being carried. I still had a distance left to fall, though. Before I could even imagine a landing. The landing came later, standing on the dais with Mother and the others. A member of a loving family with a shared vision and the makings of a new world.

When Mother asked me to take part in her new program I was shocked and excited. I hadn't been a part of the Church for very long, yet she said she could recognize a certain resolve and perseverance in me. A quality which fostered her trust. When she explained it to me, before the ceremony, I felt honored.

Standing on the dais with the others from her churches around the city, I looked out over the full congregation and knew that I had been marked for a larger task. That Janet's decision had helped me to uncover that task. It was a new and complete feeling. And when Mother stood before me and I held my hands open before her, I felt an absolute trust.

It's hard not to be excited when I talk about Mother, I explained to the woman beside me. She was crying again. She had stopped rocking back and forth, stopped holding her coat around her throat. Now, she simply stared at the open hands in her lap and cried noiselessly.

It's hard not to be excited when I talk about my family, I told her. Without really thinking, I placed my hand upon the open hand in her lap. Her fingers did not close around mine, but she did not withdraw.

The noise of the crowded room rose and fell. People left their places and returned. The movement of the nurses and interns was erratic, unpredictable. Like the dance of birds along a beach. We had overwhelmed them. The sheer number of sick and not-so-sick. Those in shock. The numbers of us who were dead. Murmurs passed through the crowd now and then. 150, 300. Maybe 400. One entire car had died. There wasn't a lot of discussion between us. Just the simple repetition of possible casualties.

The police were more methodical than the medical personnel. Two officers stood at the outer doors surveying the room; their job apparently to keep up with who had been seen and who hadn't. Moments ago, an officer with a computer tablet had approached us, asking our names, adding them diligently to his list, then moving on. A woman at the end of the hall began to scream, her voice drawing her up from the floor, up onto her feet. Her arms flailed around her as she keened. There was no husband or friend to calm her.

Someone tapped my shoulder. A uniformed officer asked me to stand and follow him. I withdrew my hand from the woman's. Her fingers remained open in her lap, her tears drying on her face. I followed the officer.

The air was cooler outside. I took a deep breath, winding my coat tighter around me. He led me toward the police trailer. Voices shouted from the left of me and I saw reporters, video cameras and microphones dancing behind a yellow police line and a barrier of officers in overcoats. They screamed questions in my direction. I did not know what to tell them.

The officer put his hand on my arm and steered me up the iron steps of the trailer. I followed him into a narrow hallway only large enough for one person at a time. At the end of the hall, he opened a door on the right and motioned me inside.

The room was small, square, gray. A simple table and

two chairs, one on either side. He took a clipboard and a pencil down from the wall near the door and placed it on the table. He motioned me toward the chair on the far side.

I completed the form he gave me and I waited, alone in the room. It was silent, warm and comfortable. I could hear no other voices. The room contained a hush which settled me, settled my thoughts and the words, images, rushing around in my head.

After the chaos of the ER, the hush calmed me and I began to relax, my body stilling in the chair. My muscles loosened and I closed my eyes for a time, placing my palms over the sockets and relishing the peace.

The door opened and an older man stepped in. He was wearing a damp overcoat. It must have begun to rain outside. Short, squat, athletic. His eyes passed over me quickly and he took the seat across the table. He drew the clipboard toward him and turned it.

He introduced himself as Detective Middleton and asked when I had boarded the train, both without a pause. I told him. He asked me where I was going, how often I rode that particular train, where I was planning to get off. I answered his questions. The entire time he stared at the clipboard before him. His eyes did not waver.

He asked me where I was standing in the car.

At the back. Against the wall. Near the rear door.

He told me that had probably saved my life.

Once the train stopped, I replied, someone was banging on the door. They managed to open it and we were able to get outside.

Middleton looked up, his eyes a silent green. His gaze, focused and direct, shocked me. He told me it was sarin. A nerve gas developed during World War 2. You can't see it or smell it, he said, and it vaporizes quickly so you don't know it's there until people start dying.

He placed the clipboard on the table deliberately. "That's what the HAZMAT guys say it was. Carried onto every car of the train in a gym bag and left on the floor at the front. See anyone with a gym bag when you got on the train?"

I shook my head.

He picked up the clipboard again and his eyes shifted away from me to the sheet before him. He read my address and phone number aloud. I told him it was correct and he moved to stand. He thanked me.

Middleton walked to the door. He stood with his hand on the doorknob. There was a low sigh and his body folded inward slightly, his tired bones working to hold together a world that was already gone.

I recognized the symptoms. Two years ago, when I was walking, there were times when the sense of apocalypse, of impending destruction, stopped me in my tracks. I would reach out blindly for a rail, a parked car, a wall. To steady myself. The world was fading out before me and I could see only a darkness, rolling on forever. That was before Mother.

In seconds, Detective Middleton regained his composure. The entire event had transpired in the instant between grasping the doorknob and opening the door. But I saw it. I knew where he was, what he was struggling with. The world had changed around him.

When the officer returned me to the chaos of the waiting room, I looked for the woman I had been talking to, but she was not there. Two Hispanic children shifted in her chair, each pushing the other, trying to claim the seat for themselves. Their mother watched, disinterested, from the chair which had been mine.

I want to tell my story. I feel I have to tell my story. If only to say, this is where I was before this morning. To understand myself before, on the other side of this event.

I find a corner. I press my back to the wall. There is no-one around me who might understand.

Something is becoming apparent. A next step. A new path. I feel the presence of the threshold all around me. All I need is to find a way to cross over. Like an explorer who has climbed upon a high plateau and gazes out over the wide horizon. Both backward to where he has been and forward to the uncharted future.

It's a stop, a rest. It stretches out flat and wide, a distance to be traversed before the next stage begins. This moment, this plateau, is significant. As significant as the morning Janet left. Or the evening I stood on the dais, open palms held before Mother. Each event a gesture toward the more complete and creative act. The act of embracing my suffering and making the world my own.

Maybe this is what I had wanted to tell the woman before. That a change is already here. Maybe this is what I see as the soul of my story and what I wanted to leave with her. I can believe for a moment that a part of it might have been carried by my words. Or maybe it was telegraphed in our touch, in the moment our hands met.

I want to touch the woman again. I want to place my hand in hers and soothe her. I want to speak to her. Partly as an expression of myself. But also because I understand suffering. I understand its purpose and its use. I understand how it can make us more complete people, how it can cleanse us. That seems important right now.

Mother helped, she pointed the way, but I did the work. The hard, mundane slog of understanding, one blind road, one small treasure, at a time. I know suffering is merely a step in transformation and that it cannot be minced around, it cannot be avoided. It must be fully, irrevocably embraced.

When Mother called us to the dais that day, the twenty who had been chosen, she was separating us. Drawing us up, closer to her. Away from those who did not understand the sacrifices and pain of change. She was marking us. As her agents in the world.

I press myself against the wall of the ER, flattening my palms to the rough wallpaper at my back. I scan the large room for the woman in the corduroy coat, but I cannot find her. I inhale slowly, pursing my lips, allowing the breath to enter my body fully. The ER has grown quieter since my return.

We have numbed. Through the trauma of the events of the train and platform. Through the inability to express to each other our horror and shock. Through the mundane inefficiencies of the hospital and police. We have closed ourselves off, away from each other, settling like individual grains of sand at the bottom of a pit. Resting beside each other but solitary.

The room has grown stale with the smell of our dirtying clothes and our sweating bodies. With tears and coughing and blood and fear. A weak heat hangs in the air and clings weakly to our bodies. New nurses and interns have arrived, called in from their families and homes, but they seem immediately blank and fatigued.

Our whimpers and sobs rise to the surface, to the edge of audible sound, then fall again. Our pain is muted now. Teenagers and children lie prostrate, limp and dozing upon the floor. The police step over them. The Hispanic children have nestled into their chair together, heads resting in sleep against one another's. Soothed by two pieces of candy wrapped in gold foil, extricated from the pocket of their mother's coat.

I want to tell my story. To finish this chapter of it. To place it within someone's hands as a gift. I want to tell someone what I have learned. But there is no-one to tell.

Standing on the dais with the others, I faced out to the larger congregation. Their attention was rapt and completely focused, completely present. I felt then that my life was beginning again. The stone had been rolled away from the tomb of my previous existence. I found myself new in a new world.

Mother stood directly before me, her back to the congregation, Miriam at her side. I held out my palm to her, upturned. Her gaze bore into me, just as it had on that first night and I knew, in that moment, that only she and I existed in the world.

With metal tongs, she reached into the pail which Miriam held beside her, withdrew a glowing, orange coal and dropped it into my open palm. "Spirit is a war with the world," she whispered, her eyes never leaving me, "this is your first wound."

I knew I could not drop her gift, could not waver. I was first in the line of twenty. I was expected to hold the gift until she had returned from the end of the line to collect it. It wasn't difficult. It was the pain of birth, bearing down with laser precision into my palm and I wanted, more than anything I had ever wanted before, to be re-born.

Minutes later, Mother collected the coal, returning it to the pail and blowing the ash from my palm. She did not say a word. She did not have to.

We didn't know each other. Those of us on the dais. We didn't know each other's names or professions. We had never met until the instant we mounted the stage together. But we understood each other. We were a part of the same future.

I did not look around me. I did not look at the line of others to my right. I stared out into the congregation. Looking down, I could see the others who did not have what we had.

Someone was throwing themselves against the rear door of the car. I could see them from the corner of my eye. They stepped back and looked around, finding the emergency release. The air was cool and dank when the door opened. It smelled of damp earth and diesel. Someone grabbed my hand, jerking me to my feet, pushing me toward the open door into the dark.

We collected out there, a few feet back from the door, muttering to each other, shuffling near the track. We could see figures ahead of us emerging from the preceding cars, we could hear their voices. Some of us were dragging the sick from the cars. We lined them against the walls of the tunnel where they coughed and cried and spasmed. After a few minutes, those of us who could walk made our way to the front of the stalled train.

The doors of the cars we passed were open. The blue light leeched out into the darkness, reflecting in dulled pewter from the chrome rails and the corrugated metal floors. In every car we could see bodies. In every car, blood.

We fell in the darkness as we walked. From fear and exhaustion. Or over each other and the rail. We massed at the front of the train. The cries of the sick and dying rolled up the tunnel toward us. We wondered whether to go further. We wondered whether to wait.

In minutes, even before a decision had been made, we saw lights bobbing at the end of the tunnel. Single beads dancing in the darkness. We heard voices, still indistinct. We could tell they were calling. We called back.

They led us out of the tunnel to the next station, the light before us glowing larger and more dense as we moved toward it. Until it blazed, hurting our eyes, as we emerged from the darkness and climbed onto the cleared platform.

They gave us water and blankets. The paramedics drifted among us, separating the sick from the well. We watched the HAZMAT team arrive. They strode down the platform in their white isolation suits and helmets, disappearing in the darkness of the tunnel. We held each other, sharing quiet words. We cried. We thought of the one person we most wanted to see again.

Later, we heard the train begin to creep slowly up the track and its nose appeared from the black of the tunnel. They stopped it at the far end of the platform. The hooded men began unloading the bodies and placing them side by side. We talked with each other or stared at the floor, trying not to look. Trying not to count.

I sat on the bench. Shaking my head. Trying to shake it of the moans and the silence. Trying to reach a place of understanding. But understanding doesn't make the truth any less terrible. The dead are safe; it's the living who continue to suffer.

I am watching the front of the car. Where the bag is. I am standing at the back of the car. From there I can see the entire space. The hair on the back of my neck prickles when the old man coughs for the first time. It feels like stage fright. I am shocked by the first objective indication that the performance has begun.

The man whose name I did not know had walked with me, entered the train with me, but I had dropped the bag at the front of the car. In one motion as we entered the car and before we turned down the aisle. Nonchalantly. As if it belonged there. No-one seemed to notice it.

Taking our place along the back wall, we wait for someone to ease toward it, but no-one does. I cannot see the bag now. There are too many people standing, swaying. Too many legs, feet, and briefcases. I keep my eyes to the spot where I imagine the bag to rest. Then the old man begins to cough. Fifteen minutes into our journey, five minutes before the next stop.

There is a silence as the train bears into the tunnel. The silence of waiting. Once the old man coughs, I feel a current in my chest, jolting outward into my limbs. A knowing. It builds slowly.

The old man coughs and the Oriental woman clutches her throat. The old man falls and a shriek rifles through the car. A woman covers her young son's face. A teenager yanks the earphones from his ears and stands suddenly. People are on their feet, peering over their seats.

The old man is bleeding now, from the nose and mouth. He loses consciousness and his limbs begin to spasm. His knees and hands striking the metal floor with the insistency of footsteps. Others begin to cough and scream and fall.

We feel the brakes grab hold beneath us, hear the rasp and the squeal. Then the overheads blink out and the blue emergency lights under the seats come up. There are more people writhing on the floor now, more people coughing as the gas makes its way toward the back of the car. Without thinking, some begin pushing backward, away from the sick, away from the blood.

The man whose name I do not know throws himself forward without a word. Climbing over those in the aisles, jostling past those in seats, toward the front of the car. Kneeling by a moaning woman who has fallen over onto her side. Righting her against a seat and wiping the blood away from her nose with his sleeve. I am left at the back. Along the wall. I believe I can see the gas moving now through the car, through the crowd. Toward the back.

I slide down the wall of the car in the blue light, my legs folding beneath me, watching the man as he moves from one person to another. I slide down the wall until

I stop. I draw my hands from my coat pockets. The old man is dead. The Oriental woman lies atop her groceries. Someone throws themselves at the door on my right. I place my hands, palms down, upon the cold metal floor.

Before April 9, we didn't know each other. We had met once on the dais, after we had been chosen. We met again at the van where we picked up the bags. We didn't speak. We didn't smile. We were part of the same family but we could not acknowledge it. Part of the same rarified group but we could not speak it.

And when the train hissed to a stop, we lined ourselves before the doors and, when the doors slid open, we lined ourselves into the cars. Spreading into the seats, the corners, standing in the aisles. Waiting collectively for the doors to close and the train to jump to a start.

We worked our ways into the larger crowd, yeast permeating raw dough. We moved with a single mind and purpose. With a will granted us weeks before by Mother. We carried its mark in our hands.

But we didn't know each other and we kept our motives and our fears quiet. Out of sight. We allowed the train, the velocity of the moment, to bear us each into the tunnel on our own rail. Separate and separated.

Once I had been lost, searching. I had walked away from a life, away from myself. I had walked to be moving. To have the illusion of going somewhere. I had been blind, yet I walked. I had walked until I was found.

The train squeals to a stop inside the tunnel. Empty again and restive, I lean against the wall. This time I'm not walking. I am a still point. This time, I merely sit quietly and allow the full weight of joy, of family, of the love we share, to bear me forward into a moment of glory where for one single and splendid instant I am absolutely one with every soul around me and the terror of it burns me clean.

Margin

Hot steel balls rattled inside Lon's skull. The dust didn't help any either and the heat baking up off the asphalt. He swung his legs slowly from the hood of the car, sliding his feet to the gravel. He flicked his cigarette into the road and, with one hand on the scalding hood, lowered his head gingerly to peer under the frame of the car for the hundredth time. The oil had slowed to a black drip now, congealing in a shallow pool.

"Damn it to hell," he snarled, kicking the driver's side tire and spinning away in disgust, facing instead an endless expanse of flat red dirt dotted by occasional scrub pine. She said she was comin', she's comin', he thought, snatching open the passenger door and reaching for the large cooler wedged into the back seat. The icy water shocked his fingers and the coolness felt good snaking up his arm. He fished for a beer, snagged it and slammed the cooler shut in one motion. He rolled onto the open door and pushed it closed, allowing his body to slant outward from the car as he twisted the cap and flung it absently to the other side of the road.

He didn't really know where he was. Must have taken

a wrong turn somewhere near Leland 'cause this didn't look like no highway and he'd hardly seen a car in the last hour. He'd done the best he could with directions over the phone but she was always better at that than him anyway.

Lon was starting to feel loose in his skin. That warm, calming feeling always hit about three beers in, turning nasty and jagged around the fifth. He woke up in the car close to 10:30, saving the motel money, the sun heating up one side of his face until it felt burnt. Until he sat up finally, muttering, "Alright, alright." He'd stopped at a convenience store for beer and ice then drove for about an hour and a half before the car seized up with a stake through its heart, staggered to a stop and bled out into the raw dirt.

He leaned against the door, neck of the bottle between two fingers, watching the heat quiver at the horizon between the far, gray mountains and the trembling sky. Feeling his skin settle into his shoes and the rest of his body rise up from there, all the way to the top of his head in those glorious few moments before the air thickened with the next beers.

When he'd drained the bottle, he looked all over for a road sign to throw it at but on this piece of shit road there was nothing, so he had to make do with a large rock thirty feet from the car. He christened the rock with green glass then watered it with the previous beers. Tugging his cell phone from his jeans pocket on the way back to the car, he punched in Peggy's number.

Five rings and the machine picked up. That uptown message of hers: "Hello, you have reached Peggy Bradshaw and it is inconvenient for me to answer the telephone at this time. However…"

"Peggy! It's Lon," he growled into the receiver, "I'm lost in hell here. Where are you? Call me."

Lon stared down at the phone open in his hand as if expecting an immediate response. He folded it slowly, slipping it into his jeans, falling back onto the hood of the car, arms spread, even though the metal scorched the skin through his wet shirt. It'll burn a little of the alcohol off, he thought to himself, squinting, trying to remember how many beers remained in the cooler.

Trip hadn't been his idea anyway. Been Suzi's. She's the one went on about starting over on the West Coast. How much Louisa'd like to see him. When he called her, told her about the car, there'd been a long silence at the other end of the line. He'd have thought she hung up but he could hear the TV sputtering in the next room.

"Suzi? Suzi, you there?"

Suzi sighed from low in her body somewhere near her ankles, "Yeah, Lon. I'm here."

"So, I'm gonna need some money, Suzi. Enough to fix the car. Or get another one. I ain't goin' nowhere in this'un."

'"Lon, I ain't got any more money to give you."

"You gotta credit card, don't you?"

"That's for emergencies. I ain't givin' you that. Gave you enough money to get you out there. That's all I had. Anymore and Donny'll kill me."

"Yeah, Suzi, but I ain't *there*. You gave me money to get there and I ain't *there*. I'm stuck in some place looks like Africa."

The television again. Oprah said something funny and everybody laughed. For a long time. Something sure as hell cracked them up.

"I don't know what else I can do for you, Lon."

He felt something slipping, like a rope he didn't have a good hold on. That sink in your gut happens when the horse gets up on you. He sighed too, so Suzi would know he appreciated his situation.

"Well, can you least come pick me up then. Goddamn car's thrown a rod."

"Lon, you're 250 miles away. Get a ride into some town and buy a bus ticket on to Louisa's."

"I ain't gonna ride no bus," Lon snorted, "Bus is for Mexicans."

Suzi sighed again and Lon gave her directions best he could. He tried calling Peggy. Then he tried Monk. Nobody was picking up their phone.

He stared down both lengths of flat, unbending road, expecting a groundswell, a tectonic shift, some event which would give the barrenness new feature. He sat down by the side of the road and lit a cigarette, extending his legs, studying the fine dust as it slipped from the edge of his boots. He couldn't be still and was up again. Feeling like a charge was building in the ground beneath him, in the sky. Some kind of electricity swirling in the dust. He paced the width of the road, kicking the rear tire of the car more violently with every pass.

Trip hadn't been his idea anyway. Something cooked up between Suzi and Louisa, his two sisters spending their afternoons between Dr. Phil and Judge Judy discussing him and his life and what he should do and how it should be done and then presenting it all to him like one big package he was supposed to unwrap and gush over like it was the best gift ever.

What the hell was he going to do at Louisa's, he asked himself, not for the first time. He'd never visited her, but he knew how her house would look. Rooms as polished as the inside of a movie. Everything in its place like it was nailed down. No place to move, no place to sit like a real person.

He could get a job out there, she'd told him. And maybe he could. Maybe he could get on at Home Depot selling belt sanders and tool boxes. Maybe they'd give him an orange vest and he could sweep up the floor when the Mexicans dropped a handful of washers.

True, he didn't have much of nowhere to go. After the last job he'd got behind on the rent and after getting so far behind there wasn't much reason to even try to catch up, so he'd just waited for the evening when he came back from The Double Deuce to find the door padlocked. He'd been on his way cross-town to Suzi's when the police picked him up. Hadn't been doing nothing, hadn't been bothering nobody. Police just bored and mean-spirited with a hard-on for him. Wantin' to take him to jail every time they saw him.

Town was as dry as a gourd anyway. No jobs, no money. He'd tried to get back on at the ranch but that hadn't happened. So, when Suzi and Louisa had it all schemed out he'd just said yes, hoping they'd give him enough money to take a roadcruise cross-country with the back seat full of beer and enough spare cash to find some ladies in a bar now and then. Instead, they'd dug up a rusted Impala with 175,000 miles and no air conditioning. Not even a tape deck. And barely enough money for gas.

Now Peggy wasn't even answering the phone and he didn't have nobody to talk to. Just the flies buzzin' round his head and the smell of old dust. Peggy wouldn't have come anyway; he knew that. Good thing he had Suzi.

Peggy was mad at him for a minute. But the TV had been an accident. He hadn't even been pissed off, just joking around when she wouldn't come over to him, wouldn't kiss him. She'd be over it soon and over her big ideas about moving to Tulsa to work at the mall.

He didn't really want to talk to her anyway. He just wanted her to talk to him. About her day down at the Quik Stop, or her brother's motel in Sapulpa, or the exotic New York hairstyles she'd seen on cable. He just wanted to hear a voice. He tried her again but hung up once the machine clicked on, barely stopping himself from heaving the phone across the field in frustration.

"Lon," the cop had said, over his shoulder through the grate of the squad car, "I'd about say you purty near used up everybody in this town."

It was that sonofabitch Andy Lapton, played tight end with him in high school. Fightin' Tigers. Class of '89. Hot shit now that he's got a gun to call his own. "Day's comin' when you're gonna step over that line from bein' a plain nuisance to a criminal and nobody's gonna bail you out then. You'll be goin' away for a while." Andy bent down, murmuring numbers and coptalk into his radio, then turned back to Lon, fixing him with a hard gaze. "You got no margin of error here, you know?"

"Fuck you," Lon barked, "you don't know me."

"That would be resistin' arrest, that kinda language, wouldn't it Tom?"

The cop driving nodded silently, with an air of misplaced sadness. Andy turned away from the grate, settling back into his seat, emitting a high-pitched leather squelch.

"Sorry," Lon had replied, in a softer tone, "I meant, Fuck you, Officer." He'd been kind of proud of that.

Things'd be alright if he'd gotten on at the ranch and they woulda hired him too except by the time he got to the office they had all the men they needed. Said they'd call if something opened up but they never did.

He'd liked it out on the ranch, up in the high hills, faraway from everything. Out there, when it got dark, it was dark for chrissakes. Just you and the livestock and a buddy or two and if you didn't wanna talk you didn't have to. You just did your work and got left alone.

He didn't drink as much out at the ranch. Not so much noise, not so much pressin' in.

But Peggy hadn't set the alarm and she said she called but she didn't cause if she had he woulda gotten up. He woulda been there and he woulda had the job. Wouldn't be in this briar patch, that's for sure. It's him oughta be mad at her.

Lon pulled another beer from the cooler. The ice was melting and the cubes sloshed around his hand like fast fish. He didn't look in to see how many were left, knowing he wouldn't like the answer. He slammed the car door hard enough to set the shocks squeaking.

A large, black crow had settled thirty feet away in the center of the road, hovering down wide wings spread, then stalking the center line before arriving at the squashed dry corpse of some unrecognizable animal, dead so long it was nearly indistinguishable from the road. The bird held the flat mass with one claw, worrying the thing with its beak, bringing up tufts of grey fur, then raising its head anxiously to glance around, head swiveling with a jerk upon its cantilevered neck. Lon rolled the bottle cap between his fingers, leaning on the road side of the car, taking a long pull on the beer now and then as the crow jerked the matted corpse from the road, digging into it with a fury now, separating layer from layer with concentration, much of its beak disappearing into the folds of the body.

In a single fluid motion, Lon flung the bottle cap underhand at the bird with all the force he could muster. It landed a good four feet to the west of its target and the bird didn't notice for a moment. Then, glancing around nervously, as if seconds were required for the creature to register sound, it spread its black wings and rose into the air.

"Damn," Lon muttered to no-one, "time was, I coulda

put that thing down." Now, he was lucky to hit a barn. Or Peggy's mom, he could probably hit her at that distance, she being near the size of a barn.

Lon shook the next to last cigarette from his pack and lit it, jostling the package, staring hard into it to assure himself no other cigarettes were hiding there. He considered stretching out in the car but, with the sun where it was, it wouldn't be any cooler, so he walked around it, scuffing the heels of his boots on the asphalt as if in the midst of a line dance, then kicking up the dust on the field side of the car.

He tried calling Peggy again. She could talk about all kinds of things he didn't care about. She could tell him what a bastard he was. It didn't matter to him. All he got for his trouble was her answering machine and the blink of the low battery light on his phone.

The beer was churning in his stomach, changing into something sludgy and dark like old blood, nearly black. It rose up into his throat and he took another swallow to push it down but he could still feel it there, churning like it was eating away at a part of his insides then running cold down his legs, the kind of cold that turns to a burn.

Lon opened the trunk of the car. Inside, three black trash bags stuffed with his belongings. He yanked one closer, tugging at the belt around the lip, opening it and withdrawing a wadded black tee. He peeled off his soaked work shirt and tossed it far into the trunk against the back of the seat. He had the t-shirt over his head when he heard the car approaching. He spun blindly, banging into the open trunk, nearly stumbling into the road.

Jerking the shirt down hard over his head, he looked up just in time to see the Lexus, long, golden, with the hushed grace of a yacht, sail by. It moved in the slow motion of a Super Bowl commercial, hissing as it passed as if hovering on a perfumed cushion of air. Inside, a woman who looked ninety, with high white hair and a red scarf loose around her neck, willing her eyes forward.

Lon stepped into the road, inches from the passing automobile's back bumper, waving his arms and shouting. He hopped from one foot to another, he danced a short jig which transformed itself instantaneously into cursing and a kind of spastic attack upon the air itself. He watched the vehicle diminish steadily down the narrow road, pumping his fist in the air, shouting curses he couldn't have explained. By the time he fell hard against the driver's side door, his t-shirt was soaked.

He lay against the door, staring up into the burnt blue-white sky, the movement of his chest the only motion as far as he could see. An ancient, dry stench lurched from the corpse which the crow had disinterred from the fabric of the road. Lon remembered the beer he'd placed on the floor of the trunk while changing shirts and stalked toward the back of the car to retrieve it, finishing it in one long pull. He tossed the empty into the open trunk beside the trash bags.

There was a storm coming. Lon could feel it, he could feel the air changing around him, the pressure dropping slowly. He stared into the horizon in every direction but saw no clouds. Yet, there was a certain stillness around him, as if the earth had stopped turning or slowed itself nearly to a stop. The scent of the car closed in, the heated rubber of the tires and their stale air, the tang of the blazing metal at the back of his throat, the range of old sweat rising from the baking leatherette upholstery. Oil, dirt, worn carpet and stale clothes; the smell of a musty suitcase left to bake in the sun.

Everything he owned in the trunk of a car which had rolled over dead and spilled its guts.

If it rained, it might cool things off, wash away the smells. Maybe it would pull the car into one of those flash floods and take it away forever, so when Suzi showed up, he'd just be standin' there with his last beer and a smile on his face.

Sometimes it seemed Suzi was all he had. She always came because she remembered all the things he'd done for her. The time he'd backed Bobby Kendricks up against a locker hard, pressing his forearm into the boy's neck and explaining every distinct mutilation promised if he bothered Suzi again. He remembered taking Suzi to the State Fair, he and Angela Hawks, his girlfriend then. Suzi had been twelve or thirteen and Angela didn't like the rides, so Lon and Suzi rode everything there together, working their way down one side of the midway and back up, from the Cyclone and Tornado to the Space Shuttle. Suzi would grab his hand just before their metal car began to rise and clutch it tightly as they were jolted into the air, her eyes growing wider, her fingers digging into his. He held her and told her everything would be alright and laughed when she screamed. Taking care of her the way a big brother was supposed to.

Something tightened in Lon's chest, clenching his hands at his sides. What should have been a good memory of the fair and Suzi had left him tensing around the center, angry with the way the present reaches back to tear away at the past. Lon pulled the last beer from the cooler, opened it and took a small sip, holding it in his dry mouth until his head cooled.

He knew she was tired and had a lot on her mind these days, what with the twins and Donny. He was a good man, just couldn't ever seem to make enough money so they were always struggling and she might have to get a part time job to get by.

He jerked the phone loose from his pocket and poked Suzi's number into it with his thumb. It rang once then blinked off, lifeless. A bead of sweat dropped from his hair to the ground near the metal toe of his boot. He tapped his foot delicately, studying the dirt, as dry as powdered blood, shifting in the vibration, settling deeper into the creases of the leather. The horizon on the far side of the road narrowed into a fade at the distance, the meeting of land and sky liquid in the heat.

Lon looked down at the fine red dust lying atop his boots, sifting into the cracked leather like fine snow, and knew that Suzi wasn't coming. Knew that she wouldn't answer his call for days. Knew that she was probably on the phone to Louisa right now.

Walking away from the open trunk, he stopped about twenty feet down the road and squatted, placing his half-empty bottle in the center of the white line at the edge of the asphalt. The air hung at his skin with the pressure of wet cloth; a pressure he noticed especially around his eyes and at the backs of his hands. The sound in his head was a dull pulse with a metallic echo hanging jagged along his spine. His jaw clenched, his teeth clamping, his shoulders tightening. He felt a smile. He knew what he wanted to tell Suzi. His shoulders released and his head floated above his neck as he reached inside the trunk for the tire iron.

The first blow sent blue cubes of glass spattering over the contoured plastic lid of the empty cooler. It thudded through his shoulders, telegraphing down his spine and into his legs, the dull pop and splatter of the glass startling him as it sprayed over the interior of the car. He hit the driver's side window squarely in the center, punching out a hole the size of his fist, then dragging the tire iron around the frame and knocking the articulated window into the seat and floorboard.

He took on the headlights next. They shattered with a gratifying explosion, hurtling glass for twenty feet. He managed to pry part of the grille away from the car before mounting the hood to swing at the windshield from above.

The fullness of his body, its electric core connecting to raw sinew and bone, spreads with the crispness of wings within him. His muscles contracted, his hands rough and raw now around the bulk of the bar, rattling in the impact of the window, the shudder jangling up his arm and slamming his bones. Sweat broke along his forehead and arms as he rained blows on the windshield with an utter physical joy. The weight of the tire iron firm in his hands, the hiss of the air as it fell, the splash of the glass. All of this while standing on the hood of the car, feet apart, swinging at the open glass reflecting open sky. All of this before falling headlong into his rage.

Minutes later, he found himself pacing in tight circles in the dry ditch ten feet down a bank from the car; stalking his circles, swinging the tire iron absently against his leg, panting, exhausted, struggling to catch his breath through prolonged coughs. His hands and shoulders burning, a cut below his left eye from flying glass, a thin stream of blood rolling down his cheek.

He struggled up toward the road, using the tire iron for support in the crumbling bank. Squatting over the white painted line, he picked up his beer, lukewarm from the sun, and downed half. His head throbbed, his bones ached. He shot a glance at the car and it wasn't doing so well either. Looked like he'd nearly torn off the passenger side door. Lon smoked his last cigarette between short sips of the beer, stretching them both out, savoring them, taking his time until he knew what to do next.

He threw open the driver's side door, being careful of the glass and punched the Impala into neutral, pulling the wheel hard to the left. With his remaining strength he threw his weight into the wedge of the door, tugging left on the wheel. His boots dug into the loose dirt and the muscles of his back raged, but once he got the car moving, keeping the momentum was easier. When the car was positioned diagonally in the center of the two lane road, he jerked it into park and brought it to a stop. He retrieved the tire iron and drove it deep into each tire, comforted as the vehicle settled onto the center of the road at the end of a sorry trail of oil and glass.

Now, anybody comin' by's gotta drive around this wreck.

Lon stood in the center of the road, heat percolating from the pavement into convection waves dissipating somewhere around his knees. The heels of his boots left faint, half-moon impressions in the asphalt when he stopped at the center line near the broken grille of the car. The crow had returned to the road, stalking sideways around the undistinguished corpse, now taking a renewed shape with its attentions. It held down the flattened corpse with one claw as it dug through the matted grey fur. The bird pushed its head into the bowels of the creature and extracted something damp and black, which it promptly swallowed.

Lon grinned at the bird and slid around the car, locking into the center line on the other side and trudging back the way he'd come. The road flattened before him in a blur, the rhythm of his boots felt steady and sure, metering the distance from the car within the two unbroken white lines. The asphalt faded into a haze with the landscape before him, his head splintered in the alcohol and the heat, his body worn with old blood and meanness.

A hundred yards from the car, he turned to look back. There was a shroud of fire dancing along the roof and hood, fine blue flame feeding on nothing, curling into the battered windows and around the door handles. St. Elmo's Fire. He'd seen it once before when he was a kid, dancing at the top of a huge oak. He'd never known it appeared during the day.

Lon watched the flames ripple down the hood and through the crushed grille, and the spectacle was beautiful, the blue sheathing the wounded black Impala, giving it color and life. For an instant, he thought the fire might transform the old car, like a magic spell from some movie he'd watched as a kid with Suzi, leaving it shiny, intact and new.

The flame dropped blue and intent onto the asphalt, then pulsed patiently up the double line. He stood immobile in the center of the road, the car complete within his attention, sensing, rather than seeing, the flame as it edged steadily toward him.

He wanted the fire to reach him, he wanted it to burn him. Burn him straight to the bone. But he knew it wouldn't matter. He knew that even if it burned him or killed him, it wouldn't change him. He would always be the same. Always the same.

Wave

for Edith

S he had wanted to say something. Something to
Emily. Emily was holding her hand.

She had wanted to call her. She couldn't remember now if she had called, she couldn't remember a conversation. There was the image of her hands holding an address book, searching for a phone number, but it floated before her, unanchored.

She is floating. She is allowing herself to float. The water flutters along the skin of the boat, its whispers rippling around her ears, her head, her still hands. Gray green rocks drift by close, close enough to touch, grizzled with lichens and deep moss. She doesn't reach out, she doesn't allow her hands the comfort of their graze. She lies still along the curve of the boat, her body rocking gently side to side in the rhythm of the current.

She is standing, a small child, on a sunlit step, wearing a billowy blue crepe dress, hair pulled back in a matching bow. The golden light is warm against her skin and she looks down at her tanned arms, her shining new shoes. The smell of spring grass, morning, and the horses.

The water unfolds itself before the bow of the boat, parting quietly, rustling like leaves. Gently, its darkened folds trace the wood in passing. Her hands are resting upon her chest, loose there, warrior-like, shuddering as quietly as sleeping doves.

Her first book. Her first night spent outdoors. Her first visit to the city. The first time she sat with him at a small cafe just off the main square. They drank cappuccino, talking about music, his eyes glittering as he explained his erotic fascination with tone. Life had speeded up then, shifted into another gradual and steady gear which carried her through years with an easy accommodation. Her first night with him. His first concert. Their first child.

The rocks tower high above the boat on either side. Through half-closed eyes she can discern the deep blue in the crevice of sky overhead. The sun out of sight. The expanse cloudless. The stone faces breathing a damp coolness into the air around her. The current quickens. She is still.

She had loosened herself into the boat, settling her tender body into the rounded hull. She had lain there motionless, receding from her skin, drawing inside, further away from the surface, from sensation. She had curled herself into the liquid center at the core of her flesh, feeling now her bones tip and roll with the motion of the boat.

The smell of the child. Her hair. Her small, probing fingers. The way a fever filled the room with the scent and heat of her. Bare legs against her own at a beach somewhere. The gift of a leaf. An unexpected kiss.

Emily holds her hand. Emily is holding her hand. It's cool and smooth along the creased blue sheet. Emily remembers the story of the ball, of her mother as a child and the ball, told often enough by her mother that it became a defining moment, a hieroglyph of her entire life.

The ball had been bright red. The color of a crisp apple. It had felt warm in her hands, heated, if only for a moment by the summer sun. It still smelled of new rubber, of course, and when she pressed her face hard into the rounded surface, hard enough to feel the resistance of the captured air within, the thick scent surrounded her.

It was impossible to say why she remembered the moment so clearly; why, in fact, she'd never forgotten it, so that she'd never found it necessary to remember. She held the ball between her two small hands, her fingers too short, her palm too rounded to keep it stable in one. She held it there and pressed again, with both hands now, to feel the pressure of her fingers struggling to meet each other through the resistant sphere of the ball.

It was a kick-ball, a dodge-ball; a little larger than a basketball but more supple, and lighter. Its surface was scored irregularly with short strokes and this scoring allowed for a better grip. It was a loose ball, having been designed for casual games where accuracy and control were less important than the gratuitous thrill of its color and the blend of dread and thrill which accompanied its contact with skin.

She sat in the back seat of the car with the new ball resting in her lap, testing its weight, its pressure and balance. She'd been extremely excited and it was impossible for her to say why. Even later, even much later in the telling of the story to Emily, she could not say what had thrilled her so on that day. She could not imagine it. But she could still smell the waxy rubber scent and the warmth of the surface in her small fingers.

She'd kicked her legs slightly on the seat. The landscape swarmed past the car window, blending gray and brown with green and blue, breaking vertical lines into horizontal, then putting them back together again. The air pressed against her, flinging her sandy hair away from her face.

Her mother, Emily's grandmother, had been angry about the ball. And she could understand, her mother had only just bought it. Her mother had yelled at her for a moment but then she simply sighed. Sitting down in the dining room chair, she pulled her body close and raked her bangs from her eyes as if they were formed of glass.

She told Emily often how she sat upon the shore of the creek and watched the ball float out of sight, its cherry-red surface catching the water's mirror and throwing scarlet into the passing branches and leaves. The ball turned and spun unpredictably as the water carried it away and she had the sensation of watching a terrific kick to left field spinning out past the pitcher in slow motion. As if she could see the currents of air parting before the surface, as if she knew all at once what it was like to be a ball, and to be spinning free.

She'd tried to call Emily. She thought she had. There'd been no answer. She'd held the phone in her hand as it rang and rang. She'd wanted to tell her something. Something about the day at the cliff where the sun burned bright orange on the horizon. Now, the idea had become too thin in her mind, spreading low like a damp mist and she could only recall the initial impulse. She felt it in her fingers, still twitching to push the buttons on the telephone. To calm her fingers, she imagined holding Emily's hand.

She is standing in her office and the last client has left. Breathing in the moment between one life and the next; between office and home, between patient and family. Her hand lies open along the dark surface of her desk, the fingers upturned slightly, collecting air or rainwater or light for later use. Feeling the breath spinning deep in her lungs. And waiting for a moment, just waiting. Waiting to begin again.

Only when the child was taller and the man had grown older in her bed did she realize that she also had aged. Lying there beside him, at two in the morning when the darkened house had stilled, with his even breath rattling beside her, she could begin to see how the leaves had closed around certain buds in her life and nurtured them quietly within her. Almost invisibly these buds had been cherished until they transformed into something like new organs: a second heart, another distinct pair of eyes, a mouth which spoke a new language.

Living had slowed, almost imperceptibly, then. The light deepening somehow, the air suddenly dense and vibrant. In her office, in the moment before she closes the door for the night, her hand lies open upon the polished oak of the desk, its surface moist and new.

The current strengthens and the boat begins to toss. Her hands have slipped from her chest and rest now, upturned, upon the dark floor of the boat. She lies motionless, nestled deep in the purple stream, a fine pale mist lowering itself around the bow as she notices the first whispers of the rapids ahead.

To look back over a vast expanse, to look back across a plane of time, to feel a constant undulating thread within her, tracing its looping path back as a single unbroken strand, sometimes knotted or snagged yet playing out backward in her vision, playing out softly, playing out behind the boat dipping now into the water just behind the keel. Back, through the mist. Back, out of sight. Out of reach.

The water lifts her, pushing up from beneath the body

of the boat, bearing her awkwardly toward the sky even as it rushes her forward, relentlessly forward. The roar of the water building like the excited breath of a lover; louder, quicker, until it is all around her, more than sound now; a touch itself.

The blue dress and the Sunday shoes, their rigid shine and flash as she walked. Her hand along the fence as the horse approaches. The touch of his finger upon her throat. The moment, one night so long ago, when the world had darkened so deeply that only tears, and more tears, would soften it at all. An orange on a table in the sun. The daughter giggling on a pony. The raging lips thundering against the skin of the boat.

She wanted a gesture, a gesture which was an acknowledgment. A kind of friendly embrace. She wanted a gesture. She tried to move her hand but it was too far away from her now.

The moment at the window. When her mother had held her close to her chest and the smell of her neck and the blue of the glass and the creak of the rockers upon the hardwood floor. The moment at the window when her daughter had pointed through the frosty pane to the deer in the meadow and had tilted her head up to look into her face. The moment at the window.

She was thinking of Emily. She thinks of Emily. She'd wanted to talk to her, wanted to tell her something. But, maybe it had happened. Already.

Rose and Thistle

Memories, like dreams dreamt by other people. They're all over me. I'm like the street sleepers on Trade Street who wear nine layers of clothes so they don't have to carry them. Occasionally they move a layer to the top, burying the dirty ones beneath. I reek of the past. It's a stain I can't scrub from my skin.

When Dawn called, it brought everything back. Picking up the phone and suddenly hearing her voice, I was somewhere else right away. The receiver became a portal from a bad science fiction movie and there I was, funneling through it with one long, gradually descending, wail.

She'd recently moved and, in the packing and unpacking, she'd found something I'd left and did I want it back?

I spun through my portal, my wail inaudible to her while a dog outside began to bark. I'm only really there for a moment, then I disappear. And I'm back to normal.

"Yeah, sure. You want me to come by and get it?"

"That'll be fine."

She gave me the address, adding that it was nice to talk to me.

I flipped the phone closed and the images tumbled
by, a whirlwind movie trailer, the kind where you know
the trailer is a lot better than the movie will be. I didn't
try to stop it. Because as long as they dipped and turned
before me I could feel that I was in one place. I'm stable
because I'm watching.

I ask Cindy to go with me, maybe we can stop by
Soup's on the way back. I ask her to drive; I tell her I
want to hang my head out the window of the car like an
English sheepdog. I watch the blur of the landscape, all
greens reds and browns, the wind in my face. Cindy
tugs on my shirt and I pull my head into the car.

"Dawn, she's that girl you did the internship with,
right? The one with the short hair and the long legs?"

"Yep, that's her. We worked in Mergers and
Acquisitions for a summer and one day it just
happened."

"What did?"

"The merging. And acquiring."

"Yeah, okay."

"No, really. She was cool for a while." I kiss Cindy
on the cheek and run my hand along the thigh nearest
the stick shift. "I like you better." She slaps my hand
and I withdraw it, returning to the window.

I like the sense of motion with my head out the car
window, the pressure of the air breaking along my face.
I squint into the wind, acceleration tears forming at the
corners of my eyes and breaking off to splat on the
windshield of the expensive sports car behind us.

I like the way the squint and the motion make
everything amorphous with only a slight and occasional
detail revealing itself at the edge of vision. Cindy tugs
on my shirt again and I fall into my seat. It's quiet and
warm inside the car, my own little rocketing womb.

"This Dawn; how long did you go out with her?" she

asks, cocking her head with the grace of a cocker spaniel trying to look endearing.

"I don't know, six months or so…"

Cindy is slowing the car as she approaches a light. I respond to the graduating motion as I would the edge of a storm; it's some kind of shabby premonition too garbled to make sense.

"So, why did you two break up?"

"Oh, the usual. We eventually found out we disagreed on a lot of things."

Cindy shifts her weight in the seat, taking advantage of our motionless moment to study me. I've slumped low, my knees nearly to my chin and I'm peering over the top of the dashboard the way I did when I was seven years old.

"Like what?" she asks, her eyes narrowing slightly.

"Like the whereabouts of Dick Cheney's secret bunker. One of us said Arizona, the other said West Virginia."

Cindy nods her head gently as she begins to accelerate, reminding me of a plastic Chihuahua in someone else's car window. "Most likely West Virginia…"

I clap my hands briskly, "That's what I thought!"

We're moving again and the world outside collapses into color once more. The storm-cloud of memory rattles up from behind but I hold out the hope we can outrun it, Cindy and I, hurtling headlong downtown, dodging a bicycle, a pedestrian.

We are together, Cindy and I, as a result of my unfortunate habit of exclaiming "I love you!" during sex. It was this generic admission which Cindy refused to let pass; in fact, she took it up as a banner, steadfastly proclaiming it a philosophy of life, building a lumpy and somewhat threadbare world around it. Somehow,

the words had awakened her from a fairy princess magic
spell and she mistook me for her Alarm Clock Prince.

She has her delusion, I have mine. I believe most of
us are only actually lucid for a few moments in our lives;
most other times we're swamped in memory or
delusion, or fading into our surroundings like a
frightened gecko. There are exceptions to this, probably
Jesus, Albert Einstein, maybe Miles Davis. But most of
us only manage to completely materialize every once
in a while. This can be comforting; in even the worst
situations, I know I only have to wait a bit before I begin
to fade, to disappear altogether, while everything else
shuffles into the past.

Cindy's strategy toward my limited awareness is to
make herself constantly present. She brings me lunch
at work; she'll often meet me on the walk home under
the guise of shopping or exercise.

She's an accompanist. It's reassuring in a way, like
having a second mother. And it works too; in the nine
months we've been together she's become an accepted
feature, like the birthmark on the back of my hand.

She's asking questions now. Asking questions, for her,
is a way of having a conversation. I've extended my
body along the sticky vinyl seat, lazily answering her
questions, staring out the window. Then, suddenly, I
stop.

It's hard to say what sets it off; maybe just the suggestion
of a gesture: an anonymous woman on the sidewalk, half-
glimpsed, and the way she raises her arm in the sun and
the way the sun catches the texture of her skin. A single
image hidden in the blur. It brings me to a halt.

I stop; that's the essential thing. And the memory
overtakes me.

Dawn and I. I'm there. She's remembering at the
same time.

"Hush…" she whispers near my ear, extending the word into a melody, "…just hush…"

We've just made love; we're still tangled in her crisp, white sheets. I'd been trying to raise myself on my elbow for some reason.

"Lie here beside me," she continues softly, her hand loose upon my bare chest. "Pretend we're kittens or something and just curl up here next to me."

Her body is the center of the room, coiled easily into the sheets, and my arms and legs are strewn around her. I'm limp and wet and in a light sweat. My face is close to her neck; I taste her on my tongue. I curl around my hand upon her stomach.

"Purr…" she suggests. I purr.

My eyelids are fluttering in serotonin overload. Her palm rests against my cheek. Her purr is even and deep. Our bodies are negotiating the greatest level of contact.

It's morning. It's a Thursday. We lie together silently for some time.

"Did you ever think…" she asks softly, her lips and breath near my ear, "about having a child? You and me?"

"You mean…"

Her palm rustles my cheek, "Don't worry, I'm still on the pill, I'm just asking."

"I don't know, I haven't really thought about it."

"Sometimes," she explains, her lips nearly touching me, "now and then, at times like this, I can feel her out there. She's just waiting for us to decide."

As soon as she speaks I know it's true.

She draws one leg up to my chest and I turn to kiss her gently. A single tear trembles in the corner of her eye.

"I even know her name," she whispers.

We fall asleep into this secret, a dream unfolding around us.

The dream has the sleepy excitement of a holiday.

Something like a grade school outing or a special Saturday morning as a child. Dawn and I sit in our flannel pajamas at the kitchen table, watching each other from opposite sides. Her bare foot rests atop mine on the floor below.

There's the steaming coffee in cups before us, the butter and orange marmalade. And the flaky croissants Dawn gets from Ollie's.

I'm studying her face now, open and calm before me. She's turned in profile, her attention to the window, the morning and the sun, as she sips her coffee. She is happy.

Later, I wake up late and rush to get dressed for work, she laughing at my panic from the swell of the bed. Later, I'll return and we'll eat Chinese from the cartons, passing them back and forth between us while we listen to Brazilian music with her cat. Even later, I'll tell her I don't want a child and it's not so much the telling as the way I do it which changes something between us.

"Do I turn here?" Cindy asks and, without thinking, I begin to unfold the instructions in my hand.

"It's the next right. On Fourth Street," I tell her, staring at my scrawl.

I'm having trouble materializing in the seat beside Cindy. I remember the old Star Trek episodes where the person beaming down would appear then disappear, appear then disappear. The rest of me is held back, lodged in the past. I can only manage to arrive in a trickle. Like a crowd behind a single turnstile. I feel the pressure and the flow.

One layer of the Onion of Memory has been peeled back just a little too far; so far I can see the tender flesh beneath and the papery layers of connective tissue. I push my head out the car window again. The rush of air strikes my face and stutters through my body and I begin to feel I'm in one place. The street is loud and garish with shops and sidewalk tables, bicycles and children.

The car begins to slow. When I fall into the seat beside Cindy I can feel my toes again. My skin, my bones, appear first; I wait for the rest of me to arrive, slowly filling the shell. Captain Kirk in the Transporter; I'm sure this is how he felt.

"What's the number?" she asks, scanning both sides of the street as she turns right. She's leaning forward over the steering wheel and squinting in the sun.

"2615."

"Should be up here on the left."

Cindy slides the car into a space not far from the entrance to the building. "2615," she chimes redundantly, "here we are." She stares up at the building, an old leaf loft converted to upscale condos as the city lurches toward gentrification. "Sweet…" she coos.

She turns toward me awkwardly, a faint smile shadowing her lips. In her own way, she's calling me back. She nudges me with one hand, "I could go with you, you want me to go with you?"

I offer her a sidelong glance.

"No, really. I could go," she insists with a smile, "I wouldn't mind seeing this Dawn."

Something thin and angular stirs within me. Something familiar.

"You can't go. Look at you," I grin back at her, "you're a balloon."

"Your fault," Cindy points out, rubbing her swollen stomach which nearly touches the steering wheel, "You put the doll in my carriage."

"You were there," I remind her. "You had something to do with it."

"That's right," she says, taking my hand and pulling it toward her tight stomach, "the first in our collection."

She kisses my fingers and I open the car door. "I'm on my way. You wait here with Monica or Ralph." I motion to the mound before the wheel and close the door.

The street is liquid around me. Everything is in motion, as if every soul in Winston has poured out into the streets at once to talk and argue, buy and sell. Five restaurants vie for the attention of my nose. Must be a Gallery Hop or something. Cindy is my anchor in this confusion; I feel a fine cord playing out between us, lengthening with every step I take.

"Don't forget," she calls through the open car window. "You promised us Vietnamese food. Me. And Julia or Howard."

I turn toward the car and smile winningly.

Maybe it would be nice to have lunch with Dawn one day. After all, it's been over two years. She's out of school now, with a real job at Wachovia. It would be fun to catch up. See how things are going.

And, even if it was a disaster, it wouldn't last that long. At least I'd know. I could wait for the moment to pass. Because every moment eventually passes, giving itself up to memory where it is safe. Where it can't touch me.

I find the entrance to the building. The noise and weight of the street dims as I begin to climb the stairs. Before I know it, I've knocked.

She opens the door and smiles. She opens it wide, then hesitates, settling into the door jamb, drawing the door back to her hip.

Her mousy hair is still cut short and she still curls it around her ears with her finger. She's wearing a white, loose-fitting blouse, open at the neck, and beige trousers which pool at her bare feet.

She doesn't speak. Her green eyes dance and her smile widens. As if she knows me.

Like the street people, I'm already moving another layer to the top.

"I just came to pick up my iPod," I tell her.

There's a silence, a silence I remember, deep and fully formed. It fills a larger space than the time it takes. Dawn's bare feet rub against one another and scuff the surface of the dark wood floor, her cuffs obscuring her ankles and heels.

"Okay, sure," she replies, her eyes flickering, "Wait right there and I'll get it."

She glances back to me before she leaves the door, parted slightly, and disappears into the apartment.

An open sliver of the room is revealed in the gap. The mid-morning light is intense through the unseen windows. There's the scent of coffee. I can see the cream-colored walls, the hardwood floor, the leg of a table.

And I just stand there. Waiting.

Roadside Tombstone

D inner is still on the table, forks overhanging plates like wilted leaves. The milk glasses are cloudy, the peas and potatoes gray, in the moonlight. The smells of the meal have jelled in the room.

The house is quiet when she opens the door, but it trembles, expectant. She eases the kitchen door closed behind her as if afraid to wake someone when there is nobody to wake. Once inside the room, she isn't sure what to do next.

She's driven for hours, going nowhere really-glad it had been pay day, glad to have a full tank of gas. By the time she returns, it is late and his truck isn't in the driveway. She knows he is gone, but not for how long.

She decides to rest for a moment, flattening her hand along the countertop near the stove. She rocks a large piece of glass on the floor with the toe of her shoe, listening to the low wheeze of the refrigerator in the darkness.

She drifts from the kitchen into the hall, careful of the mess on the floor, past the hole in the sheetrock near the kitchen pass-through. She doesn't turn on any lights, preferring the hum of the dark and its illusion of anonymity. She knows the house too well.

Her arm still aches, her head throbs. She's thankful to be alone, glad it's quiet and Tyler and Brittany are at her Mom's. She took them there after Ben raged through the kitchen, tipping the table, slamming the door-after Tyler came to her in the corner where Ben had shoved her, standing in front of his father, fists clenched at his sides. "Don't," he'd said with every ounce of courage he could muster and Ben had stopped, his own fists falling like stones. He'd looked down at Tyler quizzically-she'd had the impression she'd disappeared-then spun on his heel and roared through the kitchen, into the yard.

The house is warm and tight, its weight falling around her, gathering at her feet. Each room has its own weather and a history settling along the baseboards and into the corners like silt. The house feels oddly damp, the air smells of old dust. She floats past the arid living room, the furniture plotted around the TV, the pictures on the coffee table, the toys on the floor. Everything shudders slightly. Brittany's pom-poms doze over the arm of the couch, reminding her of the flowers and skewed cross at the edge of the guardrail Brittany had noticed earlier in the week.

"Is somebody buried there?" she'd asked, twisting backward in her seat to peer out the window. Tyler snorted his response from the confidence of his seven-year-old wisdom.

"No, no one's buried there," Beth explained. "It's probably where someone had an accident. In their car."

"But why do they put flowers there?" Brittany persisted.

"To remember the person who died."

A few things. The kid's schoolbooks. Some clothes. The cash hidden in the cracker box. She can come back later with the police for the rest. In the light, with people around her. In the light, where he can say anything he wants, snarling in the corner by the biggest officer, but he can't do anything. The officer will shake his head, stare Ben down and say, "You got no choice."

She can get her things then and maybe stay with her Mom for a few weeks until she finds a job. She'll have to put up with Mom's talking though, constantly repeating her endless lessons and observations. The late-night dinner table talk. Mom pushing a beer at her, blowing smoke from one corner of her mouth and going on about Ben—and men in general—and the constant fucking struggle just to breathe with them on top of you.

"But now you got little ones, don't ya," she'll say, like it's a revelation to Beth, "now you're stuck, ain't ya."

Money she's saved will last a few weeks anyways. She'll explain to the police and they'll nod and say she needs a restraining order but she doesn't need a restraining order, she just needs to be away, and he just needs to get his head on straight after the mess down at his job.

She finds herself in the hall and then in Tyler's room. She loses time there, stumbling in the dark over his action figures, gathering up his football gear, remembering their pride in his uniform, his team, the long pass he caught on the ten-yard line and Ben yelling beside her from the bleachers, "Goddamn, look at that boy! Would you look at that boy!"

She sits on the side of the bed trying to remember who she was before Ben, before Tyler and Brittany, trying to remember if she was anybody at all. Some girl who could've become a woman, who could've been somebody else. Some tiny sproutling attempting to push its way to the surface of the earth and spread its arms.

The earth is rolling beneath her, the walls trembling.

She makes her way to the bedroom, hand splayed along the wall to steady herself as the floor pitches. She pulls the suitcase from under the bed, throws it open on top, and stares down into it. Dust sifts into the air from the ceiling.

The rumble is steady. She listens for long minutes before she identifies his truck growling low in the driveway. She has no idea how long it's been there. With the recognition comes a tingle at the base of her spine, moving into her stomach. The truck purrs as she stands by the bed and the suitcase. Then all is quiet and the night closes around her, leaving only the rushing in her ears that reminds her of a wave constantly breaking.

The tremble has become a tremor. It enters the house from below, the walls and floor shaking harder now, the motion passing into her body.

The house is sinking, some inexorable vacuum drawing it slowly beneath the soil. The pictures rattle on the walls, the windows clench in their frames. She imagines what this might look like from the street, or from the neighbor's porch-the bicycles sliding along the yard as the soil pulls away from the hard earth beneath, drawn like a taut sheet toward the hole of the house. The grass, bicycles and lawn furniture pouring in around the sinking house like water slowly draining from the dish sink, so that when the operation is finished their lot would be scrubbed clean.

She knows he'll let himself in quietly and pad through the house without a word until he finds her. He'll stand by the truck for a minute in the darkness, his hand flat on the cooling hood, his head canted down. She's watched him from the window before, waiting. Suddenly he'll raise his head, stare out across the darkened lawn toward the swing set, then move to the back door. He'll slip quietly through the house until he finds her.

She'll feel him enter the room and she'll be motionless-hands at her sides, back to the doorway. She'll realize she is holding her breath. He'll wait for a moment by the threshold, his own breath slow and even, then he'll come up behind her, lacing his fingers over her stomach and drawing her against him, whispering apologies into her hair.

He'll still be wearing his work clothes. He'll still smell of bourbon and cigarettes but it will be different than at dinner, softer and sweeter somehow, mellowing in his body with the passing hours and the deepening night. His shirt will be damp with sweat and his body will be one strong beam of heat at her back. He'll bring one hand to her breast and she will let him.

She stands at the bed, near the open suitcase she can already see him slowly closing and sliding to the floor. A picture beside her spasms and falls with a muffled crack as the house shudders in its descent, a fine powder of earth spilling in around the window frame.

Already wet from the thought of his hardness at her back, from the thought of his wanting her, she waits for the stifled click of the kitchen door. Glad to have the pressure of his hands between her legs and the stubble of his chin rasping her neck. Glad to have the moment just before he starts and the few minutes after he finishes, when he lies on his back beside her catching his breath, sometimes resting his open hand on her stomach.

She thinks of flowers, the flowers he might bring her tomorrow when everything is okay again, the vase she'll put them in, fanning them away from the center with her palms. She thinks of the vivid blaze of the irises and tulips against the pale sofa, the pale kitchen table, the blank slab of wall in front of the bed.

Trouble in Mind

It's late in the evening and I'm lying in Bundee's narrow bed while she makes peanut butter sandwiches in the kitchen. The sheets are damp and twisted from our athletic encounter and I am tired. Tired of the things I do for my body. Tired of watching myself implicated in these weird and indefinable crimes which take place between two people.

When we met, she told me her first name. Bundy?, I asked, Like Ted Bundy? No, she replied, Bun-DEE. (Sounding it out for me.) Oh, I replied. I discovered later that her real name is Olivia Schlesinger. But, I don't let her know that I know.

She returns to the bedroom, trailing the belt of her over-sized chenille bathrobe, a mound of peanut butter sandwiches in her hand. Her hair falls in damp, red ringlets around her face and she actually looks kind of pretty. She drops into the bed on her back and I nearly bounce into the floor. Her bathrobe parts, revealing her bright pink nipples. She places the sandwiches on her chest between the nipples and they rise there like a misogynist modern art construct.

Bun-dee likes peanut butter sandwiches after sex. It's a tradition with her which seems to have its origins somewhere in her first sexual experience, but I have only spotty information regarding this event and cannot adequately address the issue. She grabs a sandwich and holds it above her head, tearing the crust off in one unfolding line. She tosses it onto the bedside table. Then, she begins to eat.

"When are you going to come home with me? It would be fun. You could meet my family."

"Haven't I already met your family?" I ask. "I'm sure I've already met them. I remember it."

"No," she replies. "You haven't met my family. You haven't met anyone."

I take a peanut butter sandwich so that I have something to do. I begin to chew. "I met someone," I assert earnestly.

"That was Molly. She was in my drama class in high school. That's the only one." Bun-dee raises up on an elbow. An untouched peanut butter sandwich slides to rest against her left breast. She's studying me now, her sandwich poised near her lips.

"I think it would be fun." She repeats this phrase constantly, a newly-discovered mantra in the cult of commitment.

"I really don't want to have this conversation," I tell her gently. "It always ends up leading to an argument."

"I don't want to have an argument," she answers and I know conflict is assured. "It's just a small thing, going home with me for a weekend."

"This conversation is not just about going home with you for the weekend," I say. I have a half-eaten peanut butter sandwich in my hand and I don't know what to do with it. The other half is presently glued to parts of my mouth and esophagus.

"You think everything is a conversation about something else," she replies, falling back to the bed and picking up the last sandwich.

"Everything *is* a conversation about something else," I tell her. I deposit my sandwich debris on the floor by the headboard. I lie down beside Bun-dee on the narrow bed and throw my arm over her bare stomach, pressing myself against her side as she finishes her sandwich.

Her pale skin is cool and her chest is littered with sandwich crumbs. I wet my finger and begin to pick them up, one by one, and put them in my mouth. Her body tremors slightly with the pressure of my finger and she laughs.

Bun-dee is fun to do things with. She enjoys good movies as well as bad ones, and she doesn't gnaw on popcorn during films like some people do. She works at Video Satori part-time and goes to school. She's getting a degree in Art History. Whatever that means. She has a giddy, liquid laugh and it bubbles out of her easily. With me, she can make the transition from serious abstract discussion to silliness or sex and back again.

I like her a lot. I even enjoy spending the night with her every once in a while. She always makes me peanut butter sandwiches and Ovaltine in the morning and it's really kind of sweet. I bring her little presents. For Christmas, I gave her an original poster for One Eyed Jacks. Lobby cards and everything.

I just have to be careful. She wants a relationship. We argue about it sometimes.

I am making tight wet circles on her chest now. Occasionally I circle an insinuating nipple. Sometimes her navel, and the silver ring protruding there. My finger traces her body slowly. It has a mind of its own.

My finger is enjoying the simple fact of skin beneath it. It likes the texture, the feel of this surface. It enjoys the way its slight pressure changes the contours of Bun-dee's body almost imperceptibly, casting shadows. My finger is operating for my entire body now, like a scout sent out to secure the terrain. And it is thorough. My finger enjoys its job.

"You shouldn't try to start a fight with me," Bun-dee whispers. "Jesus, between the two of us we're almost a whole person."

I put my lips to her ear, the scent of peanut butter and dried sweat strong around her, and that other strange smell that she gets at the health food store. I don't know what it is, but it always makes me think of tofu. I put my lips to her ear and kiss her gently. She turns her head to look at me and her face is close. Our lips are almost touching.

My lips are wired to my finger now. They are in this thing together. I can taste Bun-dee's breath, even through the peanut butter. And suddenly, for just a moment, I think I love her. I don't say a word. My lips touch hers and the hint is extremely gentle.

She opens her mouth to me and whispers softly, "I don't think you love me enough."

Recipe

Y ou got no eggs in those pancakes," Grandpa said, peering into my bowl over the top of his glasses. "You can't make pancakes less'n you use eggs."

I was standing on a chair, my apron falling around me like a curtain since I couldn't manage to tie it behind my back. I was stirring a bowl of flour enthusiastically, a fine dust building on the counter around the bowl.

Grandpa made that strange noise of his, something between a snort and a laugh. He pulled the glasses from his nose and slipped them into the pocket of his flannel shirt, coming up behind me on the chair. He let his wide, loose hands rest on my shoulders.

"Makin' breakfast for your ma?"

I nodded a curt, confident nod, brushing flour into my bangs with the wave of my hand. "She's sleeping in today. She's worked every night this week, so today she's staying in bed long as she wants."

Grandpa's hands slid down my back, fumbled with my apron strings and tied them. Immediately I felt more sure of myself. "Could you use a helper?" he asked.

"Yep," I nodded again, "you can get the eggs."

He trundled over to the refrigerator and stuck his head inside. He stayed there for a minute before coming up with eggs and milk, each in a hand. Turning toward me, he pushed the door shut with his elbow.

Grandpa was tall and thin except for a soft round belly that rolled over his belt when he sat in the chair by the TV. His hands were wide and covered in brown spots; his fingers were long and two of them were stained a yellow brown from where, Momma said, he used to smoke all the time, but he didn't smoke anymore. He mostly fell asleep in front of the TV or on warm days, on the front porch.

"How much of this stuff?" I asked, holding up the red tin of baking powder. He rustled in a drawer, digging out a tablespoon and passing it to me. "One of these, I think."

So, I stood on the chair, stirring my bowl with a grave intensity while Grandpa measured ingredients, sliding them across the counter to me one at a time. I'm sure I was talking. I was always talking. And Grandpa was nodding or agreeing with me or asking me about school and I was stirring my bowl, watching how his hands trembled as he poured milk into the measuring cup, how he squinted at the red line on the cup, how he concentrated when he cracked the egg on the side of the bowl. And now and then, he'd look over at me or I'd look up at him and we wouldn't say anything but we'd smile and every once in a while he'd rest his hand on my shoulder or my arm and I could hear him breathing, hear the slip of his feet across the linoleum when he moved, as we worked together there in the kitchen. Two people, making pancakes.

My arm was getting tired. "How'd you learn to make pancakes, Grandpa?" I asked him.

"Your Grandma, she showed me," he looked up from the cracked eggs, "you remember your Grandma?"

I nodded cheerfully, "She made cookies all the time."
"That she did."
"What was her name? I mean, besides Grandma."
"Regina Elizabeth. But I called her Gina."

I repeated the name silently a few times, my mouth getting used to the way the sounds fit together, then I tried saying it out loud: "Regina Elizabeth."

It was after Grandma died that he came to live with us. Daddy had already gone away by then. Grandpa moved into the living room because, Momma said, the stairs were too much for him. He'd brought the bed from his house and a little dresser and a small chest he kept by the dresser, but he didn't have any photographs or books or old things. He had a lot of pill bottles.

He told me little stories about Grandma as he ladled sugar into the bowl with a silver measuring cup. About how he met her at a County Dance and she was the prettiest thing there in a green checked dress and shoes with buckles. How she could ride a horse and even jump over fences. How once her wedding ring didn't fit her finger anymore she wore it around her neck on a chain. How they had breakfast together every morning and took turns making it.

"Did you love Regina Elizabeth?" I asked, because it suddenly seemed very important.

"I absolutely did," he told me and the look he gave me made me feel warm and soft and I remembered Grandma's oatmeal cookies shingled on a white plate.

The next time I looked at him he was crying. He caught my look and turned away, shuffling slowly from the counter toward the kitchen table. He angled out a chair and dropped into it with a bump.

I put down my spoon. Climbing off my chair, I went to stand beside him. He made quiet cooing sounds, his chest heaving up and down. His hands were spread in his lap and his head was down so I could see the brown spots on the top of his head.

I didn't know what to do, so big a man sobbing at the kitchen table. I'd seen Momma cry after Daddy went away but I'd never known a man could cry.

I hunched down to look into his face but it was bent too low into his chest. I thought about finishing the pancakes because everybody feels better with pancakes. Momma would feel better and he would too. In the end, I just stood beside him, church-quiet, for a long time before I reached out.

I held his hand and he let me.

Above the Rooftop

It was unusual to find her on the balcony the day she left, so early in the morning, still slumped into the baggy blue pajamas which always puddled at her feet. Her head was tilted toward a slab of spring sky between buildings, her arms clasped to her chest. It was strange to find her awake that early and outside; it was even more strange to find her still.

Elisabeth is nearly always spinning; invisible gears, their teeth enmeshed, quietly engaging other gears, or receding to a simple rotating stem, a separate axis buried deep. There are times you can see it in her hands, if you know how to look, hands haphazard upon the table except for a fine movement in the fingertips which might be mistaken for a tremor or the absent fondling of a piano.

Sometimes, I place my hand upon her shoulder and leave it there. She likes that, she says. She feels gently pressed to earth, she says, quietly seated into place. There is the moment I embrace her from behind, in a grocery store or a parking lot, arresting her forward motion for an instant, clasping my hands along her

121

stomach and easing her back toward me until my breath settles at her neck; or the moment when I take her hand, pulling her gently to a stop, to point out a singing child or a man having a conversation with himself, or a tangerine sky. There is the rooftop, my fingers spiraling the notches of her spine on the rooftop. These are moments when her spinning stops.

I slid the balcony door open and stepped out, barefoot, beside her. The morning air was cool and damp, dew dripping from the balcony rail. She didn't move, her eyes trained to the sky above and a single hawk, circling high, one block away, banking in a helix, climbing gracefully then allowing himself to fall before rolling into another turn. "I've been standing here I don't know how long," she whispered as if her voice might terrify the creature, "I love to watch him glide. I love to think of the moment he'll touch ground, only for an instant."

That's the other time Elisabeth can be still; when the world spins around her.

And today, she is the focal point of the room, her and the other guy, I think she said his name is Ron. I stand away from the activity, at the edge of the set, staking out a spot with a clear sightline, as technicians orbit the bed at the far wall where she and Ron are chatting, he bare-chested, she wrapped in a sheet. Their conversation grows more animated; her hands fanning before her, he leaning in, eyes glittering but straying from her now and then to scan the room through the glare of the lights.

Now, the clocks around her move more slowly. She settles into one spot, she comes to rest and, where she could never have repeated her lines before, now she knows them effortlessly and it's not even a matter of knowing but of entering the place where only these words would be said, in only this way, by the character she is portraying. I've helped her with her scripts for three years, delivering the opposing lines monotonously as she worked to commit the sentences to memory and I was never convinced she would remember a word when the time came. Sitting in the back rows of theatres during rehearsals as she struggled through each reading, I found a certain kind of faith for, as soon as the theatre was filled or the set was lit, she would simply change shape and become her character. When the room circles her, then she can be still.

I watched her settle into a different skin, on stage or on set, and she attended my readings; always flinging herself into the back row where she could observe the room, always engaged with others in the socializing after, always slipping me a subtle observation on punctuation or tone of voice, delivered close to my ear, her hand upon my forearm at the edge of the crowd.

"That was my wink, you used my wink," she states, one eyebrow raised, after the reading of a new piece.

I nod. "I gave it away."

She never asked what I was working on, waiting simply for the manuscript to arrive neatly clipped upon her worktable by the window and, two or three days later, a slow release of phrases, "I particularly liked…," "I wonder about…," punctuated by the occasional question or the moment she would slide onto the sofa beside me and not utter a word.

There is a terrific crash to the left of the set, the splatter of glass and a vast wave of curses that Elisabeth doesn't seem to notice. The director has wandered over and she has engaged him in conversation, repositioning herself before him, knees to her chest to secure the sheet, while she explains an idea for the scene with precise movements of her fingers. I can't hear what she's saying but Ron's gaze has shifted to another time zone while the director squats before the bed, his hand absently smoothing the sheet to her right. He nods and she smiles and he turns toward the sound of the disaster and she turns toward Ron who doggedly drags himself into the present.

It is our third or fourth date, our sixth or seventh date, it is an early date when we are still discovering syntax and idiom and she is at my place, a three room apartment in an older building on the north side of town with creaking radiators in the winter and creaking stairs in the summer and I have made spaghetti or lasagna or salad with roasted chicken and I am leaning back in my cheap dinette chair when she exclaims, wineglass scrawling a glittering arc in the air between us:

"Dessert on the roof!"

She makes the announcement, and it is an announcement, as if she has discovered a vital force of nature or a new element.

"I…" I stutter, "I don't know if there is a roof. Well, I mean, of course there's a roof but…" and I allow the sentence to slide to a rest exactly there and we drag everything with us, blanket and bottle and pillow and candle through the hallway and up the stairs to the sixth floor and a square frame on the ceiling which reluctantly disgorges a ladder. We drag it all as if there is no question we will make a place for ourselves on the roof, she trailing an old quilt I had inherited from my aunt and clutching the wine bottle, me balancing the rest in my arms, juggling it all side to side as I reach up for the rope to pull down the ladder, and we balance up the ladder, one rung at a time, steadying ourselves with our shoulders and knees, passing through a kind of interstitial realm of musty bare pine and dusty insulation, stepping along loose boards thrown over beams then pushing at a final door into a rush of cool air and a darkness peppered with stars.

And we eat Oreos with Merlot and we make love for the first time and we fall onto our backs afterward, onto the quilt, onto the still-warm tar of the roof and stare upward, neither of us speaking for a long time. And she will go home early that morning with a quiet goodbye and a single light kiss in the street level door of the building but before she goes we will float upon our dark raft beneath the stars.

And I draw circles upon her bare back. On the rooftop. She lying naked beside me, her dark hair shrouding my knee, her face turned away. She tells me stories. Of who she was or wants to be. And I brush her hair aside, away from her shoulders and neck. Slowly drawing circles with my finger, then spirals, then circles again.

Later, her toothbrush appears at my apartment, then a coat, then underwear and, finally, socks. I leave notebooks on her kitchen table and magazines with articles I mean to read. Our possessions circulate through the bloodstream of our lives settling in one location then another, passing back and forth.

And we choose ways to make this new world real. We take photos of each other and ourselves, stopping strangers in the street, handing them cameras and posing in doorways or beside street signs; we tell stories about our pasts and introduce our friends but not before telling them the story of the other, spinning new scenes from random details, arranging our snapshots into a narrative. We come round to the rooftop and the moment we touched, the rooftop and the moment we spoke, the rooftop and the moment we knew, circling around the rooftop as a mythical site which was inviolable, or the beginning of the new calendar.

She had met me at the airport the night before. I found her collapsed along a hard plastic bench at the base of the escalator, lying on her side, eyelids fluttering with the arrival of each flight until her eyes track to me somewhere in the middle of a crowd and a smile breaks through her exhaustion and she rights herself upon the bench and gently pats the empty space beside her. She's wearing her faded fatigue pants and her fuzzy pink sweater, her hair limp along the sides of her head and curling behind her ears, her mouth loose around her tongue.

I thread my arm over her shoulder and she slumps into me, "I'm sorry baby but we were on set all night, we didn't break until nine this morning and God I'm glad to see you but I'm too tired to be glad, would you carry me somewhere and put me to bed and be there when I wake up?"

"I'll even make you breakfast when you wake up. That is, if you have any food."

"Nope. No food, just bottled water and rice crackers."

In the rental car, she falls against me with the impact of a whisper, extending a finger to switch on the GPS and code the address which is, temporarily, home. I take my time with the alien roads and she talks, wanting to tell me all kinds of things but rarely managing more than a single coherent sentence.

"I haven't had time to see much of the city and the shoot goes on so long but I was hoping we could maybe go up to the...," she sighs, her hand falling to her lap; then, after a moment, "...and I think he knows what he's doing but it's hard to tell and sometimes you just have to trust something...," she appears to be studying the odometer, "...he thinks smiling is the same thing as acting...," and, nestling into my chest finally, "you smell good, you smell like you," and then she is asleep, open mouthed, quietly snoring.

I find the apartment they've rented for her, but I'm

not ready to go in yet and she's asleep so I continue to drive, in ever-expanding blocks around the building so I don't get lost; her warmth on my chest, the rhythm of her breathing, an orb of drool widening on my shirt by her mouth. The streetlights and bars and restaurants and square jowled apartment buildings slide by; at some point it begins to rain lightly and the colors smear at the windows and I realize my eyes won't focus and I turn the car back toward her apartment, hissing to a stop before the cobblestone walk.

This morning she's up, bleary eyed, stumbling around the apartment, sniffling and clearing her throat and scuffing her feet on the floor when I open my eyes from a blurry waterfront dream. She shuffles into the bathroom and closes the door and I don't see her for an hour. We drive to the set; I blink at the unfamiliar city and blatant sunlight, she is comatose beside me until we reach the house where she's filming and she disappears into a trailer. I get coffee and a donut from Craft Services and stand around listening to two gaffers argue the merits of an Argentinean film I've never seen. When Elisabeth enters the set, cinched tightly into a plush bathrobe, she is radiant.

"You're someone different when you read," she told me once, "your voice changes, you stand differently. You're you, you're just a different you." We had made love in the back seat of the car in the parking lot of the auditorium, after punch and cake and questions from the audience, and the windows were fogged and our clothes were twisted and damp and I was staring at a half-empty water bottle peeking from beneath the passenger seat. "I like sitting in the back and listening to you read and knowing that you wrote it in our apartment, in the next room. Knowing the parts about us. The parts that aren't."

It's the moment she turns over; that's when I fall in love with her. After the frenzy of climbing to the roof and falling into each other's arms, after the stories while I trace circles upon her skin; it's the moment she turns over that I see her for the first time and I fall in love with a single hard gasp and I drop my head to her stomach and angle my body across the roof and close my eyes, my head rising and falling on the crest of her breath.

I keep that moment to myself. And the glitter in her eye, visible along the back row as hot as a star, as I read her favorite passage; and her smell at two in the morning when she is submerged in dream, something sweet and salty with a hint of cinnamon. These are the memories I hold in the weeks when she is working and worlds away or when I am working and become another person or when we are separated by travel.

I nurture them for those times when we will stare at each other across the breakfast table and not know ourselves. For the moment just before she left last week, before the silent drive to the airport, her bags huddled by the front door, dinner dishes still on the table. It was late, a little more than an hour before her flight, when our passions and our arguments and our disappointments and our ecstasies tumbled together in a mammoth noisy rush to collide in the living room, tossing off sparks and heat and hard edges. We always fight before she leaves, that way it's easier to get on the plane, easier to reunite at the airport. So, when we should have been making our way to the car, instead I was stalking from room to room while she shouted about something that happened last week or last year.

Now, she is falling into herself; I recognize it from across the room. She is plummeting toward a calm at her center, she is loosening the shallow detail of the world to become another person. Ron, I think that's his name, sips bottled water and makes small talk with a set dresser, but Elisabeth has nearly disappeared, growing smaller, lighter, until she narrows to a simple instant of stillness. And I stand at the edge of her pool.

There is a sudden flurry of activity and everyone is in motion, hands fluttering with pages or cables or empty bottles. A group forms before me, shoulder to shoulder facing the bed and, just as suddenly, a quiet descends, all noise burning off the set like morning dew until the stillness of the room matches Elisabeth's low tone and everyone is hushed and breathless.

She wriggles a shoulder from her sweater and my hand sweeps her shoulder blade, the grit of the cookie mingling with the tang of the wine as I try to swallow. We drank Merlot then, from the bottle as we couldn't accomplish glasses, and she pulled Oreos she'd collected in the kitchen from the pockets of her sweater. Later, she turned onto her back and I lay down. I told my stories then and something changed in the telling.

I told my stories then, her fingers feathering my hair slowly as if naming each strand; so, the rooftop appears now with each flash of her bare shoulder in the bathroom mirror, or the flare in her eyes at a joke, or her fingers drawing a receipt or a key from the pocket of her coat. I imagine a bird lowering from the edge of a convection wave toward the dark platform of the rooftop where two people lie naked on an old quilt, their pale bodies floating in the dark like a secret constellation.

From the sudden silence of the room, Elisabeth begins to speak, her voice gentle and low, a whisper of intimate distance. She doesn't glance back to Ron, her eyes focusing on the memory opening before her. She tells him a story about herself at twelve, the death of her father and the tears of her mother, downstairs at night, soft tears she could hear upstairs in her bedroom. She tells him of the small cards and presents she left for her mother, on the kitchen table or on her dresser or under her pillow; small things she made for her every day for a year, until the anniversary of her father's death when they walked to the stone together and cried together, holding each other in the spring grass. And she cries as she speaks, soft tears slipping down her cheeks and dropping to the sheet beneath her. She tells him the story as if it were metered from a dark edge of her soul, as if it were actually happening, and she doesn't miss a word.

The people before me are motionless, as if cast in wax. Ron kneels on the bed beside her. The boom operator inches toward the bed, his feet slipping noiselessly along the floor, his arms held high. The camera glides in slowly from the left on an extended arm with the grace of an insect probing a new bloom.

I recognize her intimacy; the slow elaboration of each sentence as a sensual transaction. The world has narrowed to the pool of the bed and his body beside her; her voice gently deflects everything else. Her words form a surrender and she discovers her faith. Ron doesn't speak; his fingers along her spine forming an answer to the question she hasn't yet thought to ask.

Now, she is enacting our life, motionless upon the bed at the center of the set, her flesh warm beneath Ron's hand, tracing lazy circles down her spine. Her sentences begin to take on the rhythm of those circles upon her skin. His finger spirals gently between her vertebrae and when he reaches the last, she turns over naked before him and he peers down into her eyes as if seeing her for the first time.

Ron's hands hang above her open body. He is motionless. She is silent now, waiting for him to speak. Her breath is shallow and quick and a blush rises along her chest. Ron's hands find themselves and his fingers brush her breast. I cannot see her face but I know her expression.

Elisabeth has touched ground, just for an instant. She has etched a new feature of our life onto the restless sprawl of the world. She is making another part of who we are real with the same diligence and care as I present this story to you.

STEVE MITCHELL has been a construction worker, cowboy, substitute teacher, chef, and has developed and managed a mental health program for the chronic mentally ill. He's worked in theatre, film and multi-voice poetry. His work has been published in the *Southeast Review*, *Contrary*, *Glossolalia*, and *The North Carolina Literary Review*, among others, and has been nominated three times for the Pushcart Prize. His short story, "Above the Rooftop," was named a storySouth Million Writers Award Notable Story of 2010, and he is currently completing a novel, *Body of Trust*. He has a deep belief in the primacy of doubt and an abiding conviction that great wisdom can inhabit very bad movies. He has an ambivalent relationship with his cat, Mr. Zip. Sometimes, he just doesn't know. And that's all right.

Cover Artist PETER TANDLUND is one of the founders of Comigo, a consulting and business services company in Sweden where he works as a web and graphic designer. He is also a songwriter and musician in the Swedish alternative-pop band Trabant. When Peter is not working or playing music, he loves to go on long walk and take photographs with his Diana F+, Holga, Flexaret, or iPhone.

Peter says of the cover image, "Lately I have been experimenting with long-exposure photography, trying to find new ways to create movement and blurs with a painterly feel to them. When I take this kind of shot, I leave the shutter open for 2-4 seconds while walking. As with all image making, I think about the composition and try to find subjects and objects that are interesting in shape, color and contrast. The thumbnail view in a camera's viewfinder is a great aid for composing: the small window lets you focus on the important elements of the image."

You can find more of Peter's work at www.flickr.com/ petertandlund, and follow him on Twitter at twitter.com/petertandlund. His band's website is trabant.nu, and Comigo can be found at comigo.se.

CPSIA information can be obtained at www.ICGtesting.com
Printed in the USA
BVOW032047120613

323185BV00001B/3/P